A YULETIDE MYSTERY

KEITH FINNEY

Flegg
Publishing

1

8:10 A.M. CHRISTMAS EVE

A higgledy-piggledy assortment of frost-covered thatched roofs glistened in the bright morning sun in the quaint Norfolk village of Stanton Parva.

Postman Ian Toleman stepped carefully along the cobbled pathways to deliver the last of many greeting cards he'd pushed through a variety of letterboxes since early December.

"I bet you'll be glad to see the back of Christmas, Ian?"

Patting the near-empty postbag, he smiled at his fellow villager. "Only another half a dozen and that's my lot for two days." He cupped his hands together and blew a stream of warm breath over his numbing fingers. "I'm getting too old for this game, Terry. Two more years and that's me retired, and I can't wait."

Terry Rawlings laughed as he half turned to pick up a pint bottle of milk from his open-sided delivery truck. "You think you have it hard. Fancy handling all this freezing glass through the winter, and customers who maintain I'm to blame for robins and blue tits nicking the cream from the milk."

The postman smiled as he pushed two envelopes through a narrow Victorian letter plate, taking care to keep his hand clear of the spring-loaded flap. "Get away with you. You're nowt but a youngster. How old are you, thirty-five?"

Terry sighed. "I wish; I'm forty-one , if you must know."

"Not to worry, then. Only another twenty-five years before you get your pension. Buck up, lad, it'll soon be Christmas."

Wishing each other season's greetings, the two men offered a cheery wave and continued with their morning routine.

At the other end of the narrow, winding street, a couple emerged from a flint-faced house, their breath condensing in the chilly morning air like steam escaping from the kettle.

"Are you sure you've got everything, Lyn? There will be no time to come back with so much going on today." Anthony Stanton looked back at the village's head teacher before letting out a yelp as he slipped on the frost-covered pavement.

"Serves you right. You're always in such a rush and preoccupied with whether I have or haven't remembered something. Next time, mind your own business, and watch your footing instead of me."

Ego and backside bruised, he scrambled to his feet, looking around furtively to check whether anyone had seen him fall.

"And you reckon you aren't vain? Don't worry, there's nobody around to notice you making a fool of yourself. Now, if you're ready, let's get to the garage."

Ant chuntered to himself as he dusted the frost from his trousers. He gave his companion a look of disapproval.

"Don't look at me like that. You may be the lord of the manor's heir, but don't try that aristocrat thing with this lady." She playfully wagged a finger at her companion as she linked arms. "Since you're not safe to be out on your own, I guess I'd better keep a tight hold, or we'll never get to your parents' Christmas bash."

As they navigated around ice-covered puddles, they enjoyed the cold, crisp morning air as a midwinter's sun bathed everything in its mood-lifting embrace.

A lone voice penetrated the otherwise still morning. "Can't you two leave one another alone for two seconds without all that kissing and cuddling malarkey?"

The tattered sign above a rickety wire fence read Fitch's Automotive Services, and the voice belonged to its owner.

"Have you nothing better to do than spying on your customers?"

"Someone got out of the wrong side of the bed this morning, or was it that tumble you've just taken?"

I knew someone would notice.

"Morning, Fitch, I see you're your usual bright self when normal people are in bed."

The mechanic grinned as he showed himself to his two oldest and best friends while rubbing oil from his hands with a grubby cloth.

"As you say, Ant, normal people would be in bed. It's only a fool like me that will open up on a Christmas Eve to fix his best mate's car. One more word and I'll shut the place, meaning you two will have to walk to the Hall, and I can go grab a bit of shut-eye."

Lyn nudged her accomplice and whispered into his ear. "Don't blame Fitch for you falling over and being in a foul mood. I have absolutely no intention of walking to your parents' place, Christmas or not."

"Bah humbug! Scrooge had the right idea."

Lyn shook her head at Ant and let go of his arm. "Never

mind, Lord Misery-Guts, you know what he's like of a morning even without playing Tumble Tots for all to see. Did you fix his silly car? I told him, no heater, no get in."

Fitch looked around the disorganised garage forecourt and pointed at a frost-covered vintage car in the far corner. "All fixed, and next time, don't fiddle with things you don't understand."

Rather than bite at his friend's gentle rebuke, Ant shuffled to his beloved Morgan. "We'd better get going, or we'll be late for breakfast." He looked back at Lyn, busy exchanging a shaking of heads with Fitch.

"That's all right, Anthony Stanton, no need to thank me for saving your bacon and shoe leather. What are friends for after all?"

Rather than acknowledge his friend's sarcasm, Ant unlocked the car door to retrieve a windscreen scraper.

"He really doesn't like mornings, does he? I'd forgotten just how ignorant he could be before he's eaten." He glanced at Lyn sympathetically.

She shrugged her shoulders. "He can please himself. But if he doesn't buck up soon, he'll get more than kedgeree for breakfast, I can tell you."

Before Fitch could respond, the Morgan's powerful engine rumbled to life as the vintage vehicle slowly made majestic progress to the garage forecourt entrance.

"See, yet again, I'm waiting for you. Are you going to jump in or what?"

Lyn turned back to Fitch. "I swear I'll swing for him one of these days. Don't forget, his father has invited you for lunch, so don't be late."

Fitch nodded and gave a cheeky smile. "See you at one and good luck with him." He nodded towards the Morgan.

Wearing a resigned smile, Lyn chose her steps carefully

as she walked around the back of the car, opened the passenger door, and folded herself into the tiny vehicle.

"Come on, Captain Happy, let's get a move on before you go into a complete decline—but watch the roads—they'll be treacherous with all this ice."

The Morgan sped up out of the village, leaving only a temporary trail from the exhaust to hint at its presence. Meanwhile, Fitch locked the ramshackle iron gates of the forecourt to avoid further interruption and made his way into the relative warmth of his small office.

Clearing the last of Stanton Parva's mediaeval surroundings, Ant pressed a little harder on the accelerator, revealing Norfolk's flat landscape in all its glory. Left behind were the thick stands of elm and oak, shorn of leaves, instead their branches covered in a thick layer of crisp white frost. Now, a patchwork of meadows and ploughed fields nursing their young crops offered a beguiling glimpse into a world that hadn't seemed to have changed in centuries.

"I'd like to arrive in one piece if you don't mind."

"And I would like my breakfast. I'm starving."

Lyn shuffled in her seat. "Talk about a bear with a sore head, just watch out for ice, and don't forget we promised your father we'd call in on Percy."

Lifting his foot from the accelerator a little was all the acknowledgement Lyn needed to confirm he knew she was serious.

"Heaven knows what state my uncle will be in this time; you know what these professor types are like. Do you remember having to coax him out of that tree?"

Her memory of the old man's eccentric habits caused Lyn to giggle. "I never could work out how he got up there at his age. All I can say is thank heavens it was summer. I hope he doesn't try it this time, or you'll end up with a frozen relative with his arms wrapped around a tree branch like a sloth on a go-slow."

A few minutes later, the Morgan turned right across the Norwich road and into the Stanton Estate. A porter's lodge stood sentinel on each side of the entrance, their long-gone residents leaving the ornate stone structures looking forlorn.

"I've never understood why Percy doesn't stay at the Hall since the cottage is only a stone's throw away."

"Uncle Percy likes his own space. I suppose it comes from spending so much time at the Bodleian Library at Oxford University during his research. Anyway, we're here now; let's see what awaits us within."

Bringing the vintage motorcar to a majestic halt outside the front gate of the chocolate-box cottage, Ant sprang from the car before tussling with a garden gate, which took several attempts to open.

"Give him a knock."

"No answer. Do you think he's already at the Hall?"

Ant shrugged. "I suppose he might be, although you know he's a man of habit, so if he was told we were calling, he'd have waited. Is it locked?"

Lyn twisted the weather-beaten latch. To her surprise, the door opened with a creak. "It feels like an episode from the *Addams Family*. It might look like a picture postcard, but this place gives me the creeps." She stepped through the half-open door and glanced around the small, dark living room, its low ceiling and exposed beams adding to her sense of foreboding.

"Well, have you found Percy?" Ant had finally won his battle to close the gate and stepped gingerly along the frosted pathway.

One fall a day is enough for anyone.

"What was this place used as, anyway? It's hardly big enough to take your coat off in."

"We have used it as guest accommodation for as long as I can remember. Dad told me it housed the head gardener and his family."

Lyn stepped through an open doorway into the tiniest kitchen she'd ever seen. "Family?"

He laughed. "Believe it or not, one Mr Albert Thorpe had a wife and four children. Cosy, don't you think?"

Lyn shook her head. "I suppose that's one way of putting it. Anyway, back to Percy. He must have got fed up of the damp or whatever that sickly smell is and decamped to the Hall. At any rate, he isn't here."

Ant looked towards a steep, narrow staircase. "Let me just give upstairs a quick check to make sure he's not still in bed, although from memory, Uncle Percy is an early riser."

Gripping an unstable wood handrail as if his life depended on it, Ant carefully ascended the creaking construction. A few seconds of silence fell as he checked the two rooms that comprised the cottage's upper floor. "Nope, not here, and his bed doesn't look as though Percy slept in it because it's strewn with all kinds of papers. I'm coming down."

"Watch your step, young man. I intend to deliver you to your parents in one piece and in full working order."

Ant laughed as he navigated one step at a time but still stumbled on the final tread. "Thank you for your applause, and for my next trick..." He held his hands wide as if waiting for applause, having stayed on his feet.

"I think you mean next trip. Will you behave yourself and—"

"Wait a minute, there is something not right here."

"What do you mean?"

Pressing his forefinger to a small rusty wall hook, he dashed outside before returning a few seconds later. "Uncle Percy always hangs his car keys on that hook and his car's gone."

———

LEAVING THE COTTAGE AND CLEARING THE SMALL WOOD IN which it stood, the full splendour of Stanton Hall at Christmastime came into view.

"Doesn't it look superb?"

Lyn stopped walking to take in the picture-postcard sight of the mediaeval hall decked in Yuletide decorations and frosted Christmas trees. "You're right, it's beautiful. All we need now is snow, and it'll be perfect."

"Then you'd better close your eyes and make a wish, Lyn Blackthorn. Meanwhile, we'd better get inside, and find out what happened to Uncle Percy." He grabbed her hand and pulled her gently towards the front entrance.

Passing through the heavy double doors of the old building, they saw a constant stream of staff and family members crossing each other, some holding yet more decorations, others excitedly chatting about the party to come.

"Have you seen my father, David?"

The butler stopped what he was doing and turned to the Earl of Stanton's only surviving son. "I believe the earl is with the rest of the family in the drawing room, Lord Anthony."

He thanked the butler and headed across the black-and-white-tiled hallway, leaving Lyn in his tracks.

"Some things never change, David."

The butler smiled courteously as she followed her oldest and closest friend.

A chorus of greetings met the pair as they entered the intimate room with its Regency decor of brightly striped wallpaper, pastel-pink friezes and satin-upholstered furniture.

"Happy Christmas and great to see you all."

"And the same from me too," added Lyn.

Making their way through a sea of smiling faces and friendly gestures of kinship, the pair sought, and finally found, the Earl of Stanton.

"There you are, my dear son. Lyn, how you, my darling? I suppose he kept you waiting as usual?"

Lyn pressed her lips to the earl's cheek and brushed his skin with an affectionate peck. "You know your son as well as I do, so I think we need not pursue the point further." She winked at the old gentleman and returned his gentle smile.

"When you two have stopped besmirching my character, perhaps we can return to the matter in hand."

His father narrowed his eyes, causing his bushy grey eyebrows to merge into a continuous ribbon of spiky hair. "It is Christmas Eve, Anthony. Not the time for giving your father such a serious look, perhaps?"

Suitably rebuked, the son relaxed his facial expression. "Apologies, Father, but it's Uncle Percy. He isn't at the cottage. Have you seen him?"

The Earl of Stanton let out a weary sigh and shrugged his shoulders. "Where has my wayward cousin got to this time, I wonder? I left the man looking through the family archives in the armoury last night. The man made such a fuss over dinner about his silly research that neither your mother nor I could wait to get shot of him."

Lyn raised her eyebrows.

"Don't look so surprised. My father and Percy have an accord. Uncle Percy doesn't bang on about the Hall's history, and Dad keeps his views on academia to himself. Last night the accord seems to have broken down."

The Earl of Stanton attempted to get up from his armchair.

"You just sit there, Gerald. There's no need for you to go anywhere."

The elderly gentleman responded with warmth to Lyn's gentle touch as she placed a hand on his shoulder. Resting back into his sumptuous chair, he fixed his eyes on his son. "There comes a time when one has to choose between loyalty to family and enjoying one's Norwegian salmon. Last night Percy crossed the line. As I say, the last I saw of the man was in the armoury."

Ant's enquiries ended when his ten-year-old nephew Timothy pulled at his arm. "Uncle Anthony, is it true you are a spy?"

The earl patted an arm of his armchair and gestured the young boy to sit. Gently taking hold of the youngster's hand, he looked deeply into the boy's eyes and pointed to his son. "Because he's a spy, he can't tell you he's a spy, get it?" The young teenager nodded conspiratorially. "The thing is, we all are to keep it a secret, otherwise we'll blow his cover, and, well, anything could happen. And we don't want that, do we?"

The young boy looked at his Uncle Anthony, who was touching the side of his nose with a finger and furiously shook his head.

"That's the ticket, young Simon. Now, I suggest you go grab another piece of chocolate cake. Remember, you're in on the secret now, so scouts' honour, dyb-dyb and all that. You must not say a word in case hostile forces overhear you."

Young Timothy shook the earl's hand as a sign of honour amongst gentlemen before heading for the chocolate cake, all the time scouring the room for the enemy forces his elder had warned him about.

"You're a tease, Gerald."

The earl patted the arm of his chair again to indicate Lyn should take Timothy's place. "Another fifteen years, and he may follow in his uncle's footsteps, heaven forbid." The old man looked up at his son, whose smile dimmed.

"Not if I have anything to do with it, he won't. Anyway, back to Percy; is it time to call the police?"

His father at first shook his head. "It's Christmas Eve, Anthony. The police will think we've gone barking mad, especially when I have to explain it won't have been the first time my eccentric professor of a cousin has done a runner." He looked to Lyn for support.

"You have a point, Gerald. The thing is, his car's gone. That must mean something?"

"And it doesn't look as though his bed has been slept in," added Ant.

The Earl of Stanton scanned the room as if looking for divine intervention. "At least look in the armoury, and get the staff to check as many rooms as they can. We don't want to go bothering the police only to lead them on a wild-goose chase. My influence only goes so far, Anthony."

————

"So you've examined the cottage and this building?"

Detective Inspector Peter Riley wasted no time in cutting to the chase as he spoke to the earl, his son, and Lyn in the cosy atmosphere of the library.

"As I say, Peter, and by the way, I can't thank you enough for coming out on Christmas Eve—yes, we've looked everywhere. There's not a trace of him." Ant handed the inspector a cup of tea from a side buffet table.

"The man is a buffoon at times. He's also full of his own importance, but it is strange that he left, if indeed he has, without first saying something."

Peter Riley stopped drinking momentarily as he digested the earl's words. "You seem a little irritated if I may say so, my lord."

The Earl of Stanton shuffled position in his leather wing-back chair. "He is a silly old fool, and it's against my better judgement that we have bothered the police. However, the top and bottom of it is that my silly cousin has disappeared off the face of the earth."

Lyn stepped away from the open fireplace, where she'd been gazing into the flames of the crackling logs, and knelt by the earl's side. "We can rely on Peter to find him, Gerald. Despite what you've just said, I know you. Now you mustn't worry, do you hear?" She stroked his arm as the earl gave her the look a man who'd always wanted a daughter of his own might offer.

"Just one more question, if I may. Why was Mr Long-barrow staying in an old workers' cottage in the first place when you have so many rooms available here?"

Ant answered for his father. "Peter, they have never got on too well. It's that love-hate thing you often get between family members. The other reason is that his own brother, Cedric, is here for Christmas. They argue like cats and dogs as soon as they set eyes on each other. Percy, being a research academic, seems to enjoy his own company, so it was easier all round to put him up in the cottage."

The inspector listened to Ant while never taking his eyes off the earl. "My lord, I wonder if you might explain—"

The sound of a police radio crackled to life. Inspector

Riley patted his suit jacket to check which one he'd put it in, before lifting the small device to his ear. "I see. Yes, immediately. Disturb nothing, do you understand? Over and out."

All eyes fell on Peter Riley, whose expression had stiffened.

"We are receiving reports of an incident at the lake."

2

10:26 A.M. CHRISTMAS EVE

The winter sun hung low in the mid-morning sky without the power to make much of an inroad into the heavy frost. Stanton Lake was a hive of activity as police divers and their backup crew got ready to head out into the icy waters.

"Not the great place it was when we were kids, is it, Lyn?" Ant shuffled his shoes on the covering of fallen leaves as they crunched beneath his feet, causing a dusting of minute ice particles to form a wind-blown mist.

Lyn ambled down to the shoreline, arms folded as she watched a police boat make its way towards a dark object in the middle of the large lake. "The hours we spent playing pirates down here, eh? It seems so long ago now, especially given the reason we're standing here right now." She continued to stare into the middle distance as her companion joined the sad vigil.

Minutes passed slowly as police radios crackled to life and then fell silent. They watched Inspector Riley arrange several police constables into a straight line, each holding a long cane. "Take it slow, you lot. I want every leaf turned;

every bit of wood moved so we don't miss a thing. Right, off you go."

Anthony Stanton watched as two police divers slid from the small boat and approached a floating object.

It's like a scene from a TV show. This is crazy.

"Do you think it's him?"

Lyn half turned, her arms still firmly crossed. "I hope not. Doesn't that sound awful, because if it's not your Uncle Percy, then it'll be some other unfortunate soul. One way or the other, a family will miss one of its own this Christmas."

Suddenly a diver waved his arms above his head. Ant watched him turn back to the boat where a policeman knelt over the vessel's side, talking to the man in the water.

A split second later, police radios all around came to life. Ant turned to see Inspector Riley with the palm of his hand across one ear while listening intently to the radio with the other.

Come on, what's taking so long?

The line of police officers stopped scratching around in the undergrowth as Inspector Riley turned and shouted, "Stand down, it's a false alarm."

He looked across to Ant, smiled, and nodded. Lyn grabbed at her friend's arm to get his attention before giving him a hug.

"Thank the Lord for that. It's bad enough to lose a loved one at any time of year, but on Christmas Eve, it would've been heartbreaking, don't you think?"

Ant reciprocated her affectionate hold and gave a sigh of relief. "You've never said a truer word. Come on, let's get out of this place."

As the pair retreated from the water's edge, Ant shouted his thanks to the police officers and shook Peter Riley's hand. "Bring them up to the Hall for a cup of something hot and a bite to eat, will you, Peter? I hope you got your invitation for the party this evening?"

The detective inspector's eyes opened wide. "That's so kind of you, Anthony. My boys and girls will be thankful to get out of the cold. As for the invitation, yes it came early last week, and thank you, I'm delighted to join you."

The men shook hands as a parting courtesy, and while the detective relayed the good news to his staff, Ant and Lyn linked arms and wandered into the woods.

"Let's walk back to the Hall across the estate, Lyn. We can leave the Morgan here. I'll pick it up in a day or two. I need to clear my head."

She made no complaint as they crunched frozen leaves underfoot and held the occasional small branch aside so they could pass, causing a spray of frost crystals to swirl in the chilled air.

"I know it sounds obvious, and I'm so glad your Uncle Percy wasn't in the water, but it begs the question of what *has* happened to him?"

As they cleared the treeline and broke into open countryside, he shrugged. "I'm baffled, but unless he turns up, we have to assume he's got himself into a scrape."

A comfortable silence fell between the close friends as they strolled, arm in arm, across the crisp grass which hid beneath its wintry covering. Slowly turning to their right, Ant caught sight of Stanton Hall. It was a vista that never ceased to make him catch his breath.

What a place it is. I'm so lucky.

Squinting to avoid being blinded by the morning sun, both attempted to shield their eyes.

"Let's head back into the trees. It will take a few minutes longer, but at least we'll be able to see where we're going."

Lyn's hand almost collided with Ant's cheek as she

turned sideways while still shielding her eyes. "So you're suggesting we swap getting lost in a maze of trees for being blinded by that thing." She pointed towards the sun without looking.

"Sounds about right. Come on, but it'll be colder in the shade, so put your collar up."

Passing from the bright morning sun into the semi-darkness of the trees, a quietness enveloped them. From time to time a lone bird or squirrel scurrying about in the branches caused a dusty cascade of frost to float lazily in the still air.

"This place is spooky enough during the day. I wouldn't like to be out here in the dark."

Ant released his hold on Lyn and wailed while holding his arms above his head like a cartoon ghost character.

"That's not funny, you stupid man. If you don't behave, I'll leave you in here to entertain whatever wildlife is daft enough to give you the time of day."

Suitably chastened, he lowered his hands and adopted a look that Lyn was more likely to come across on the guilty face of one of her pupils.

Reaching out, she linked arms with him again, giving Ant a gentle tug to remind him who was boss. "Next time I'll —" Lyn stopped in her tracks.

"What's the matter?"

Lyn pointed to her left. "Somebody's watching us."

Ant looked around. "I can't see anyone, you must be—"

His sudden silence startled her. "So you can see her too?"

Ant didn't respond at first. Instead, he squinted and moved his head from side to side trying to get a better view. "Oh, I don't know. Wait, yes, she's over there. She'll freeze out here just in that dress. Let's see if she needs help."

In a split second, the figure disappeared.

"What do you think of that? How strange. Anyway, it's

cold enough without searching for an imaginary woman larking about in the woods. Come on, let's get going."

Lyn was having none of it. "Hang on a second. We both saw her, so we can't have imagined it."

Anthony strained to look around for a second time. "There's nothing here, Lyn. I agree, we both saw something, but it doesn't mean it was a person. It was probably a trick of the light. We've searched. If there had been someone, we would've at least found a track, but there's nothing."

———

As they entered the dining room, lunch was in full swing with members of Ant's extended family engaged in lively debate and laughter as they tucked into their buffet meal.

The earl ambled over to the doorway. "Inspector Riley has told us the splendid news; at least we know my silly cousin hasn't drowned."

Anthony offered his father a half-smile. "It still means he's missing, Dad. He could be anywhere. Has Uncle Cedric arrived, because if he hasn't, we need to get in touch and let him know his brother's missing."

Before the Earl of Stanton could reply, the formidable figure of Aunt May joined the conversation. "I rang him from home yesterday. He said he was just leaving, so should have arrived late last night. I rang again this morning. I got no answer, so assumed he was on his way. The problem is, he doesn't own a mobile, so we've no way of getting in touch."

Lyn turned to the earl. "You mentioned nothing about Cedric, Gerald?"

He stroked his chin between two fingers. "Actually, I'd

forgotten Cedric was due last night. I heard Percy arguing with someone on his mobile. I assumed it was his brother, as usual."

Inspector Riley interrupted the conversation as he entered the room with two constables, who had been checking the immediate grounds for any sign of Percy. "Do you mind if these two get a warm by your fire—they're freezing."

Lyn took the initiative and gestured for them to move towards the cavernous Adams fireplace. "I don't suppose you came across a woman dressed in an old-fashioned dress, did you?"

The two young bobbies gave Lyn a confused look before shaking their heads in unison.

"Has somebody else gone missing?" asked Inspector Riley as he moved his gaze between the earl, his son, and Lyn.

"Not at all, Peter. Lyn and I were walking through the woods a little earlier and thought we saw something."

"You mean someone." Lyn glared at her best friend.

The earl chuckled. "Was she dressed in purple?"

"How did you know?" Lyn's astonished response caused an immediate silence to fall across the room. "What?" She turned her attention back to the earl.

He took a few seconds to compose himself. "We call her the Lady in Purple. That's her." He pointed to an oil painting high on the wall. "Newly married to the second Earl of Stanton, she disappeared from this very room. Over the centuries, she has appeared running towards the house several times, each time when a member of the family turns out to be in danger. You remember last time, Son?"

Inspector Riley and Lyn looked at Ant.

"What does your father mean?"

The seconds passed in silence.

Why do we have to drag this up again?

"It was when Greg had his accident. My father maintains he saw her just before the police rang to say my older brother had died." Ant fell quiet, losing himself by looking into the dancing flames of the open fire.

"So that's why you were so dismissive in the woods?"

He didn't answer.

The room remained silent as unfolding events sank in. No one spoke nor lifted their eyes from the deep-pile Persian rug that enveloped the floor.

Inspector Riley's police radio broke the unnatural quietness. Turning the volume down, he listened. "Roger that."

He turned and whispered to the earl. "Good news, sort of. We have had no reports of vehicle accidents so far this morning. While this doesn't solve the conundrum, we can at least rule out one scenario."

The Earl of Stanton gave an almost indiscernible nod in acknowledgement of the detective's news. "As you say, Inspector, as you say."

Just as a murmur of conversation filled the room, it ended abruptly for a second time. Heads turned and worried glances were exchanged.

Lyn turned to the earl. "What on earth is that? It sounds as if someone's..."

———

FITCH'S JOLLY DEMEANOUR DISAPPEARED IN AN INSTANT AS HE breezed into the drawing room. Unable to understand the sea of frozen faces, he turned to Anthony. "What have I done now?"

His unintended levity did the trick in snapping people

out of their stupor. However, the earl continued to exchange worried glances with his son.

"Sorry I'm late, but at least there's plenty of food left. May I just dive in?"

Lyn held out a hand to Fitch. "I think I'll join you, if only for a stiff coffee."

"I assume that comment makes sense to you."

Seconds later, Ant joined them at the buffet table. "What took you so long?"

Fitch was, by now, filling his bone china plate with a host of Christmas-themed treats. "Er, oh, they look nice. What did you say?"

"Late, why are you late?"

The mechanic finished filling his plate. "I was helping Dr Thorndike start his car. It's getting colder out there, and he was desperate to start his house calls. His car had other ideas. Anyway, I got him going."

Pricking his ears at mention of the doctor, the earl wandered over. "Well, I hope he completes his house calls and gets over here pronto, because he's got my medicine."

Inspector Riley joined the foursome. "Time to look around the cottage, I think. Do you two want to join me?"

Five minutes later, all three passed through the picturesque cottage's front door, with Riley having dispatched two constables to look around outside for any traces of Percy Longbarrow.

"How old is this place, Anthony?" Inspector Riley scanned the tiny living room.

"As far as we know it's as old as the Hall, so over five hundred years. It appears on every plan we have of the estate."

Peter Riley took a particular interest in the oak ceiling

beams, lowering his head each time he passed under one to avoid banging his head.

"Didn't you say the Roundheads damaged it in the English Civil War?" said Lyn.

Ant nodded. "Yes, they did. The family supported Charles I. They were Cavaliers. Oliver Cromwell and his New Model Army took offence, chucked us out and set fire to the place."

"Then how come it's still here, including your family?"

Ant gave a throaty laugh. "Luckily for us, though it may sound strange to you, the Hall wasn't defendable. That meant Cromwell didn't waste time blowing the thing up like Corfe Castle. The fire caused some damage before the locals put it out. After the civil war we had to buy the estate back. My father maintains Cromwell and his cronies ripped us off. It left the family broke for well over a century, but we didn't have much choice. It was a case of start again or let the place go to rack and ruin. You can imagine what that would've meant for the village."

Peter Riley's interest in history intensified. "I thought you were Church of England, not Catholic?"

Anthony smiled at the detective. "It wasn't about which faith you followed. That said, the family we won the estate from were Catholics. It seems they had a tough time of it under Elizabeth I and King James."

There's more to Peter than I've given him credit for.

Riley suddenly slipped as he stepped onto a small rush mat in the centre of the room. Before either could reach him, he tumbled backwards and hit his head on the stone floor.

"He's out of it. That was a heck of a wallop, Lyn."

She knelt next to the inspector. "He's unconscious; we'd better get an ambulance."

Ant joined his companion and felt the back of the inspector's head to identify any swelling. "This blood isn't his."

Moving Riley into the recovery position meant that they could lift the old mat to one side, which revealed its secret.

"Look at all that blood. It doesn't look good for Uncle Percy."

3

1:32 P.M. CHRISTMAS EVE

Inspector Riley murmured incoherently as he regained consciousness.

"What's he saying?"

"Dunno, Lyn. He won't know where he is for a while. Give me a hand to help him sit up, will you?"

The injured man instinctively reached for his head as his two rescuers gently supported his back.

"What happened? Why am I on the floor?" Riley attempted to get to his feet.

"Hang on a minute, Peter. You've taken a nasty fall and hit your head. Just sit there for a minute until you have your wits about you. We don't want you falling again."

"The carpet moved, I slipped." Riley slowly looked to his left. He panicked. "There's blood everywhere, what have I done?"

Lyn quickly took hold of his hand and gently squeezed. "It's okay, it isn't yours. You have quite a big bump, so we'll need to get you checked out at hospital, but you have lost no blood, I promise."

For a few seconds Riley seemed to accept what Lyn was saying. Then he began to murmur incoherently again.

"He's in shock, Ant. Let's get him onto the sofa and try to keep him calm. I'll make him a cup of tea. Do you want one?"

"I wouldn't mind a coffee."

Having settled the unsteady detective into the aged chair, Lyn disappeared into the tiny kitchen, leaving her companion to act as nurse.

"How are you feeling now? Any headache or dizziness?"

Riley slowly tilted his head back, while massaging his neck. He winced in pain. "I've had better days, I can tell you, but I'm not feeling too bad."

Ant stopped Peter from rubbing his neck too vigorously. "Just be careful. We don't think you've damaged it, but let's not take any chances, eh?"

Lyn ambled back into the petite lounge carrying a small floral-patterned tray on which sat three drinks. "Here's a nice mug of tea for you, Peter. Be careful, it'll be hot."

She made sure the detective had a firm grip, before handing Ant his coffee.

"Are you sure this is coffee?" He scratched his nose as he looked into the steaming brown liquid.

"I'll give you a slap. Next time you can make your own drink."

What did I say?

He decided not to retaliate to what he considered an unnecessarily harsh rebuke for asking a perfectly reasonable question. Instead, he concentrated on the inspector. "Feeling any better?"

Riley nodded, then immediately moaned as he massaged his neck.

"Well, that was a clever thing to ask him, wasn't it?"

Ant let out a sigh as he gave his best friend a sideways glance.

"Don't you look at me like that, Anthony Stanton. Anyway, how long do you reckon the ambulance will be?"

I give up.

"I don't know, what did they say to you?"

Ant immediately knew from the confused look he was getting from her that something had gone terribly wrong. "You rang them, didn't you?"

As Inspector Riley sat back in his chair groaning, Ant relieved the detective of his china mug to avoid it spilling into the policeman's lap. "This isn't good. I thought you rang for the ambulance."

He could feel Lyn's eyes burning into him without the need to turn around.

"You know full well I was in the kitchen. I assumed you'd put the call through. This is awful. You had better ring them straightaway; he's still in shock. I'll nip upstairs for a blanket to keep him warm."

As Lyn scurried up the steep staircase, Ant scrambled for his phone and tapped the keypad.

Damn, the signal's rubbish.

He ended the call and tried again, this time with success. "Yes, that's correct, about four hundred yards after you turn off the road into the estate. You'll find us on the left."

As Ant finished his call, he watched Lyn scurry back down the stairs. "For goodness' sake, don't you fall as well."

Lyn ignored his plea as she continued her descent at a furious pace. "Here, help me get this over him. Wrap it tight."

Seconds later, Ant stood back to admire his work. "He looks like one of those Aztec mummies." Pleased with his observation, he chuckled to himself.

Lyn squinted. "You do say the daftest things, Anthony

Stanton." She hesitated for effect. "I think he looks more like a Christmas tree. That blanket has quite a lively pattern, don't you think?"

A moment's silence fell as they exchanged mischievous grins, which morphed into laughter as Inspector Riley began to murmur again. For a reason neither could understand, it made them giggle even more.

It wasn't long before the emergency ambulance arrived. Within seconds of hearing the vehicle's tyres crunching on the frozen trackway, the cottage door opened and in walked two paramedics.

"The poor man is as white as a sheet. What happened?" The female medic, dressed in a green coverall with various bits of equipment stored in the tunic's many pockets, knelt in front of her patient.

Lyn recapped recent events. "And so, we thought we'd better get him comfortable."

The male paramedic, a man of around forty-five with a waistline to match, spotted the blood Ant and Lyn had discovered previously. "That isn't from him. What's been going on here? Perhaps I should call the police."

Ant moved quickly to explain the situation.

"I see," responded the man. "In that case, we'll leave that side of things to you. Meanwhile, we need to get the inspector to hospital. The doctors will want to check him over. He might well look worse than his injuries turn out to be, but because he fell into unconsciousness and still looks spaced out, we shouldn't take any chances. I imagine the hospital will wish to scan him to rule out anything serious."

As the medics wheeled the detective out of the cottage, he started to shout. "My dog, what about my dog? I have to get home."

Lyn ran out of the cottage to reassure him they would see to his dog.

Within minutes, the medics had Riley safely secured within the ambulance and had left the Stanton Estate.

Ant glanced around the tiny room.

It looks like a battlefield clearing station.

Lyn, meanwhile, immediately set about clearing away various bits of bandage and sticky tape. "You mentioned earlier that Percy's bed had papers all over it, but did you see what they were?"

Wary that it was a trick question, Ant answered with caution. "No, not really."

"You were telling Peter Riley about this place appearing on every plan you own of the Hall. Well, most of the papers are said plans."

Ant stroked his chin with an upward motion. "What in heaven's name was Uncle Percy up to?"

Lyn took a sharp intake of breath. "Whatever it was, perhaps someone found out and didn't like it one bit."

———

"Yes, I know it's Christmas Eve, but it's critical I find out who he was talking to." Ant pressed his case to the intelligence officer from whom he desperately needed a favour. "Anything you can find out will be a great help. I have to know what happened to Percy."

Lyn frowned. "Do you think he will help?"

He placed his hands together as if praying. "Jeremy is an expert in telecommunications and is at the top of his game. If he can't find out who Uncle Percy was talking to the night he disappeared, then no one can. I've called his mobile until I'm blue in the face. Either he switched it off, he hasn't got it anymore, or the battery's flat. None of which helps us find the man."

Lyn placed her arm around Ant's waist and snuggled into him." We'll find him. I'm sure of it."

"Now, then, have you two nothing better to do than canoodle in my hallway?" The Earl of Stanton smiled as he watched his son return Lyn's affectionate gesture. "I have the perfect distraction to take your minds off the disappearance of my silly cousin. May I ask that you entertain your Aunt May? She's driving everybody potty being her usual bossy self. One thing, though, whatever you do, don't mention Percy. To say they hate each other is an understatement. You'll find her in the long gallery."

Ant raised his eyebrows but obeyed his father's instruction. Climbing the ornately carved dark oak Jacobean stairway, Ant shrugged his shoulder at Lyn, who was following two steps behind. "This should be fun—not. Now that Dad has warned me about not mentioning Percy, you know what will happen."

Lyn gave him a weary smile. "What you mean is you'll do what you always do in ignoring your father's advice and get yourself into another scrape."

Ant shrugged as he reached the wide landing of the old staircase, waited for Lyn to catch up, then opened the door to the long gallery.

"These were such a good idea, don't you think?"

"I assume you mean for the gentry, Lyn. Yes, being able to promenade up and down one of these things while it's pouring with rain outside is a great idea. I suspect the servants thought differently, having to lug heavy logs for the fires up all those stairs."

A long, narrow room stretching more than a hundred feet in front of them lay ahead. The outside wall contained hundreds of small glass panes, which allowed natural light to flood the otherwise dark space. Along the inner wall, three huge open fireplaces kept its occupants warm as they exercised during inclement weather.

Portraits of family abounded, and at the far end of the gallery, a glass-topped library case exhibited signed letters from four monarchs, spanning two hundred years from 1480.

The formidable Aunt May sat on a low, wide, silk Regency chair to one side of a roaring log fire. "Ah, you've come to keep your poor aunt company. How kind, please, do sit down." May twisted her ample frame and nodded to show where her visitors should sit.

It wasn't long before Ant commented on the amount of tutting his aunt was indulging in. "Is everything all right?"

The elderly lady placed her needlework across her lap and utilised a thumb to point over her shoulder, without bothering to turn around. "They are the strangest creatures; do you not agree?"

At the far end of the gallery, several children were running around excitedly.

"What, the children?" replied Lyn.

Aunt May picked up her needlework and recommenced a section of delicate stitching. "I say only that the child catcher featured in that wonderful documentary, *Chitty Chitty Bang Bang* had the right idea."

Her visitors exchanged astonished glances. "But Aunt May, that was a fictional film starring the American, Dick Van Dyke. It wasn't real."

May set her needlework down in a single snappy manoeuvre. "Are you sure? At any rate, children always seem to take the moral high ground and believe things are true or untrue, black or white, and that no middle ground exists. I find this a distasteful habit, which is not to be encouraged in young people."

Lyn bristled. "You mean until adults teach them that it's fine to lie and cheat, to be deceitful and take joy in judging others?"

Ant sucked air between his teeth as he waited for his redoubtable relative to retaliate.

"Well said, young lady. I can see why my nephew and you get on so well, since at least one of you has the strength of character to set their position out confidently without fear or favour. Anthony, you'll learn a great deal from Miss Blackthorn, if you have the sense to open your ears, that is."

He blushed as Lyn revelled in Aunt May's assessment.

There'll be no living with her now.

He moved May's attention in a new direction. "How about a game of cards?"

The suggestion was met with a ferocious glare from his aunt. "Are you mad, boy? There will be enough of that nonsense this evening. For now, I'm content to continue stitching my tableau and embarrassing you in front of your young lady. However, you may pour me a whisky." The elderly lady pointed to a silver tray on which sat a lead crystal decanter of single malt and a matching pair of cut glasses.

"Don't you think it's a little early, Aunt May?"

He received a second cold stare for his troubles.

"Don't be so pompous; you have too much of your father in you. Now, please get me my drink. After that I won't detain you. I'm sure you can amuse yourselves elsewhere."

As the pair left, Lyn turned. "It's no wonder she never got married and had children. May is quite a tyrant when the mood takes, isn't she?"

He smiled. "I know it's a terrible cliché, but her bark is

much worse than her bite. I've always had something of a soft spot for her."

Lyn looked astonished. "What?"

"She's not what she seems. When she was twenty-one, Aunt May's wedding got stopped just as vows were being exchanged. She apparently never showed interest in anyone else. Dad has hinted that Percy had a hand in things but never explained exactly what happened."

Lyn shook her head as they descended the grand staircase. "No wonder she hates Percy."

———

"Now, how did you get on with May?" A sheepish smile spread across the earl's face as he welcomed his son and Lyn into the larger of the Hall's two drawing rooms. The adults gathered around a roaring fire as several children scurried about playing tag.

"Careful, children, there are one or two pieces in here older than the Hall."

The four youngsters halted momentarily, looked around the exquisitely decorated room, then continued their game.

"My father used to say the same thing to me when I played cricket in here. I had one or two close calls, I can tell you."

Lyn playfully wagged a finger at the earl. "So that's where your son gets his mischievous side from."

Ant adopted his misunderstood schoolboy look, which cut no ice with Lyn or his father.

Turning the fire embers with a long wrought-iron poker, Ant caused sparks to fly in all directions as the sudden infusion of oxygen gave the log fire a fresh burst of energy. Replacing the ornate poker into its stand, he turned to his father. "What happened between Uncle Percy and Aunt May?"

His father held an open palm towards his son. "Let's not go there, Son. Some things are best left unsaid, and I speak as one who has the scars to prove it. Now, my dear, let me explain who these ugly creatures staring down upon us are."

Ant knew when to surrender and contented himself watching multicoloured flames dance in the huge dog grate.

He must know he's shown Lyn those pictures a dozen times before.

"And so we come to the infamous second earl. You remember me telling you about his unfortunate wife a little earlier?"

Lyn stroked a hand of the man she considered almost a father. "Yes, I do, Gerald, but I never get tired of you telling me about your family."

The earl patted Lyn's hand. "You're so gentle with an old man, my dear. How lucky we are to have you in all our lives."

On the other side of the room, the children continued their game of tag at a feverish pace. "Can I play?" shouted Ant.

The children squealed with delight as one of them launched himself at his uncle, touched his elbow, and shouted, "You're it," before making a run for it to rejoin his companions.

Ant played his part with gusto as he set off in pursuit of his lively nephews.

Phew, I'm not twenty-one anymore. I'm jiggered.

Taking delight in outpacing Uncle Anthony, the young ones split up and ran in different directions, making his task more difficult.

"I'm getting closer. Who shall it be? Yes, Timothy, you're the one." Ant put on a spurt and almost caught the young lad when, at the last second, Timothy feigned a move to the left, then jumped to his right, leaving his pursuer to fall over the arm of an exquisite leather-upholstered chair.

Ant sat down to catch his breath. Before he knew what had hit him, the youngsters were on him. "No tickling. I hate being tickled." His protestations fell on deaf ears. "If you don't behave, I won't tell you about the ghost." The children froze and looked at him expectantly.

Thank heavens for that. Time to tell a tall tale or two.

"Come on, Uncle Anthony, tell us a ghost story, it's Christmas after all," said Timothy in a breathless voice.

Ant closed his eyes for effect and held his hands above his head, fingers pointing to the richly decorated plaster ceiling. "I call on the spirit of Christmas Past to reveal himself." He opened his eyes to see four sceptical faces looking back at him.

"We read that book at school, Uncle. It's called *A Christmas Carol*," said young Helena, leaving her elder with no doubt about her disappointment.

This lot's too clever by far.

Fortunately for Ant, a sudden gust of wind caused a loose windowpane to rattle. He took full advantage of the gift. Rapidly closing his eyes and clenching his fists, he sat bolt upright. "Is that you, Old Nick? Show us a sign you're with us."

This time the act gripped them with anticipation. Examining their facial features, he wasn't sure whether they were about to laugh or cry.

Better rein things in a little.

"Is he here, Uncle? Can you see him? You know, Old Nick."

Ant lowered his voice to a whisper. "Shush, now, no loud talking or you'll scare him away."

Timothy was having none of it. "Uncle Anthony, shouldn't that be the other way around? You know, isn't he supposed to frighten *us*?"

The lad's compatriots looked at each other and then at their uncle with a unity of purpose.

Time to think on my feet.

He gripped the arms of his leather chair and stared without blinking at the blazing fire. "He's here: can you see him?"

The youngsters' mischievous smiles changed to ones of apprehension. Ant had a second piece of luck when the windowpane shook again.

"Now who's frightened of whom, I wonder?"

In an instant, all four jumped on their uncle and hugged him, their laughter tinged with nervousness.

"Is Old Nick really here, Uncle Anthony?" squealed Timothy.

Ant tickled the four youngsters until they were almost crying with laughter. "No, he's gone. He whispered to me he was hungry and was off to the lamp shop for a light lunch. Ah-ha, get it, lamp shop, light?"

A communal groan erupted in acknowledgement of their uncle's poor joke.

Suddenly a thud rattled the chimney. The children immediately stopped laughing and looked to their uncle for reassurance. Instead, the earl stepped in. "If that's Father Christmas, his watch needs checking."

The children exchanged worried glances before relaxing into a fit of giggles as the old gentleman's joke sank in.

A split second later, a second bang preceded something dropping into the grate, causing an explosion of sparks to erupt from the fire. Ant jumped up as he spotted something bouncing from the fire and rolling across the hearth.

Stepping briskly across the spacious room, he peered over the leather-topped club fender and reached down.

"What is it, Uncle Anthony?" said Timothy with a measure of apprehension.

Now what do I do?

He had hesitated for as long as possible. There was only one thing for it.

"It wasn't Father Christmas. It was Old Nick. Can you believe it, he's lost his head? Which means it's not so much about him having a light lunch as feeling a little lightheaded."

Ant lifted the scorched skull from the fire hearth and held it up for all to see.

The children at first screamed, then collapsed into fits of laughter.

"That was a good joke, Uncle Anthony," squealed Timothy.

Meanwhile the earl, Lyn, and Ant exchanged looks of bemusement.

4

2:46 P.M. CHRISTMAS EVE

Relieved that his young charges found the bouncing skull hilarious, and that he'd had planned it all along, Ant closed into a huddle with his father and Lyn to inspect the macabre object.

"For something that's been up a hot chimney for heaven knows how long, it's strangely cool, don't you think?"

Lyn took hold of the remains and ran her hands across its surface. "Well, it's been out of the fire for a few minutes now, Ant, so I wouldn't expect it to be hot to the touch. However, I'd have thought it would've shown signs of scorching. Soot is one thing, but there's a complete absence of burning."

Like a scene from pass the parcel, the earl now took ownership of the fleshless object. He, too, ran the palms of his hands over the skull as if he were rolling dough to make bread.

The old gentleman paid particular attention to the back of the bony artefact, halfway between the crown and where it attached to the neck. "Yes, I thought so. Did you feel this,

Son?" He turned the skeletal remains and pointed to a slight bump.

Ant nodded. "Do you have it, Dad? I assumed I'd had some accident or other when I was little."

Lyn leant forward to check what the two men were talking about.

"It's genetic, my dear. All the male line has this minor bump on the back of the head. That means this poor chap is one of us, though who, is quite another question."

The adults hadn't noticed the young ones listening in. "I also have one," said Timothy as he gently prodded the back of his head.

"And me," shouted Rupert excitedly.

"That's not fair," muttered Jennifer. "Boys always think they're better than us. I want one too." The young girl continued to probe her head for any sign of an unusual bump.

Lyn made a point of addressing Jennifer's complaint. "Don't worry, the tables will turn when you grow up, just you wait."

Both boys gave Lyn a confused look. Nine-year-old Jennifer smiled enigmatically.

"Come along you lot, I have a feeling Cook may have several bowls that require icing licked from their interior. Fall in a straight line now, that's right. Left foot first on the count of three, follow me."

The earl marched his charges smartly out of the room, leaving Ant and Lyn in sole control of their boney relative.

If ever we find Cedric, the skull will be a puzzle concerning a long-gone ancestor he will be keen to solve.

The quiet interlude didn't last long as several members of staff entered through the open doorway.

"May we, sir?" asked the first to enter.

"Mary, yes, please carry on."

Without making further comment or acknowledging their employer's son held a human skull, the team began preparations to dress a long table at the far end of the sumptuous room.

"Don't you think that's a little pretentious?"

Anthony raised his eyebrows. "You're a snob, Lyn Blackthorn. I assume you're referring to the table being made ready for the family's gift-giving this evening?"

Lyn narrowed her eyes as she prepared to counterattack. "I'm not at all snobbish. Normal people receive their presents on Christmas morning. Except the Royal Family, who I know do it on Christmas Eve at Sandringham House. Why do you have to copy them?"

Ant laughed as he absentmindedly placed the skull on an adjacent chair as if it were an everyday occurrence. "You call yourself an academic and you don't know that it's a long-standing tradition in Scandinavian countries to do as we do. I think someone needs to go back to school, don't you?"

"Listen here, Lord Know-It-All, I—"

Lyn's verbal assault ended when the butler, David, appeared in the doorway. "Sir, Mr Cedric Longbarrow has arrived. Shall I show him in?"

"Absolutely, David; I need to talk to him straightaway."

The butler gave a slight nod and withdrew.

"At least your Uncle Cedric will put one mystery to bed and explain where he's been all this time."

Ant nodded as he moved the skull from the leather armchair onto a nearby shelf to avoid it being inadvertently sat on.

A few seconds later, the butler reappeared with Cedric. "The Honourable Lord Cedric Longbarrow."

He strolled lazily into the room, hands in pockets. "Alas, poor Yorick, I knew him well." He pointed to the skull and laughed.

"Uncle, you well know that is a misquote and what the Bard wrote was, 'Alas, poor Yorick, Horatio, a fellow of infinite jest, of most excellent fancy,' et cetera, et cetera."

Cedric let out a belly laugh. "I'm pleased to see your parents sending you to that inordinately expensive school provided a positive return. And how are you, my dear?"

Cedric closed in on Lyn, took hold and gently kissed the back of her hand.

"Always the charmer, Cedric. However, this time that smile of yours won't get you out of trouble."

Cedric kissed Lyn's hand for a second time.

"I told you, your schoolboy charm will only take you so far. Now, where have you been? Anthony and the rest of the family have been out of their mind with worry."

The new arrival shrugged his shoulders before turning to Ant and extending a hand in greeting. "You have my irascible brother to thank for my late appearance at what looks to be excellent Christmas preparations. I think the Hall looks splendid, unlike poor Yorick."

Anthony squeezed his uncle's hand, ensuring the man's attention. "What you don't know, Uncle, is that Percy is missing. He arrived as planned, but no one has seen him since late last night."

"And why does that not surprise me in the least? That man is a buffoon, a selfish prig and cloaks his lack of thought for others under a mask of eccentricity."

Cedric withdrew his hand from Anthony's firm grip and placed it back into his trouser pocket.

Lyn shot him a stern look. "This is serious, Cedric. We have the police involved. The least you can do is show some concern for your brother."

Oh dear, light blue touch paper and stand back.

Cedric's cheeks flushed and the tip of his nose took on a purple hue. Ant could see, though concealed, his hands had contracted into fists.

"My dear Lyn. You know I have the greatest affection for you, and the big galoot standing next to you. However, as for brothers, you have no experience of the frustrations such a relationship brings with it. Tell me this, has his car gone?"

Ant gave Lyn a sympathetic glance.

He's reeling you in.

"Er," she hesitated. "It has."

Cedric clapped his hands, momentarily startling staff decorating the table. "I knew it, he's probably taken off on one of his little adventures. I suspect he's come across something in those dusty books that he always has his head in. He gives no thought to the chaos and worry his meanderings cause. My brother is a stupid, selfish man and that's all there is to it. Now, point me to the food, I'm starving."

The harshness of his uncle's words took Anthony by surprise. "I understand how frustrating it must be for you, but we're concerned for his safety."

Cedric shook his head. "Which brings me back to answering your original question of why I'm late. Yesterday morning, my dear brother rang to ask that I make a minor diversion on my way up from Hampshire. He prattled on about some wooden beads he needed for his research and since it was on my way, could I do him a favour."

Lyn's eyes lit up. "You spoke to him?"

"My dear, with the greatest of respect, that is what I've just said. In fact, my telephone felt like a hotline to the

Kremlin since I had only just come off the phone from speaking to May. Anyway, I duly set out and would you believe it, the place was closed. Then a snowstorm blew in, so I hunkered down for the night."

Cedric's companions exchanged incredulous looks.

"What, in your car? I'm surprised you didn't freeze to death."

"Anthony, my dear boy, as you know I too was Special Forces, so it won't surprise you that kipping in temperatures a few degrees below zero is of no particular hardship. I always carry a sleeping bag, torch, dry biscuits and several personal hygiene products to survive any eventuality. It was snug, actually,"

Lyn shook her head. "Except that May told us you don't carry a mobile 'on principle,' whatever that means, which meant you may have been snug while we worried ourselves to death."

Cedric brushed Lyn's concerns aside. "My dear, owning one of those modern contraptions means that nosy people can disturb your peace day or night. I have no need for such an abundance of human interaction. Now, I want some cake."

———

CEDRIC'S PROGRESS ACROSS THE MAJESTIC HALLWAY DIDN'T GET far before being interrupted by an incandescent May. "So there you are. Like your brother, you're a disgrace. You are both untrustworthy and not worthy of being part of this family."

The ferocity of the woman's attack took everyone by surprise. Lyn and Ant tried to intervene, while the family members looked amused and staff diplomatically averted their gaze to continue trimming an enormous Christmas tree at the bottom of the grand staircase.

"Why must you continue to remonstrate about something which happened over forty-five years ago? My brother did what he did. As I have said many times, I had no part in his actions. I had no forewarning, and he has never fully explained his motive. Will you please cease using such poisoned language, which continues to debilitate so many innocent people. I must warn you, May, let it go, or else."

Cedric bounded from the public space and disappeared down one of the many long passageways of the Hall.

"Don't you just love Christmas with the family?" whispered Ant into Lyn's ear.

"It beats that episode of *Dallas* they always show on TV over Christmas; you know, the one where Bobby Ewing comes out of the shower."

Anthony shook his head at Lyn's obtuse comment. He turned to inform the staff that all was well, and what they had just witnessed was only the first instalment of the usual pantomime that would play out over the coming days.

Within a few seconds it was over. May had taken her leave heading up the magnificent Jacobean staircase, while other family members who'd witnessed the lively scene resumed eating mince pies.

"Talking about Percy, why don't we head to the armoury, seeing as that's the last place he visited."

"Anything for a bit of peace; lead on Macduff," replied Lyn as she prodded her companion in the shoulder to get a move on.

Although a relatively small space, the armoury's extensive display of seventeenth-century steel breastplates and helmets hanging on the stone walls did little to make it less cluttered.

Several rows of dusty wooden shelves containing family archives and an ancient pine table, strewn with parchment and bedraggled ledgers, completed the scene of general untidiness.

Lyn gingerly sat on a three-legged stool, which Ant warned had a fearsome reputation for tipping its occupants onto the floor without notice.

Moving a long-disused pewter quill-pen rest and inkpot out of the way, she pored over dozens of rolled-up parchments, unfurling each one and weighing the edges down with lead weights made for the purpose.

"What are you hoping to find?" He had been in the room dozens of times over the years and what Lyn seem to find fascinating, he found boring, given none of it was new to him.

"As you said, Percy was in here for a reason. He's a history professor and a renowned Research Fellow. That man knew what he was looking for before he disappeared. All we need to do is find out what it was."

"Is that all?" He turned from Lyn to examine the old armour hanging in menacing rows above him.

Now, where are the ones with musket-ball dents in them?

After spending several minutes inspecting artefacts and remembering the happy times, he and his older brother had spent playing Roundheads and Cavaliers in the Hall's extensive grounds, he heard Lyn murmuring.

"What did you say?"

Lyn pointed to the margin of a parchment. "Look here in the margin. Someone has made a note. Do you think it's modern?"

Anthony sauntered over to the table and leant over Lyn's shoulder. "No, you can tell from the script that its old. Anyway, no one would deface these precious things, especially not Uncle Percy. Can you read what it says?"

Lyn moved her head closer to the faded document. "It's a name. Owen, I think?"

"Let's see." Ant placed a hand on Lyn's shoulder gently guided her to one side a few inches. "It looks like 'Owns' to me."

Lyn shook her head. "No, it's definitely Owen. The question is, who is Owen and why would only his first name appear in the margin?"

Anthony straightened up and scratched his head. "Beats me. Perhaps he liked to tag things, you know, like modern graffiti artists. One thing you can check is the date; all these documents carry one. Can you see it?"

Lyn paid particular attention to the top and bottom margin of the ancient document. "Yes, there's one here. I reckon it says 1559. Just think about that, Elizabeth I had been on the throne just twelve months. Isn't that fascinating?"

He shook his head. "I can't imagine Uncle Percy was looking for autographs. Perhaps he—" Anthony cut himself short and turned to the heavy Tudor-arched door. "I think someone is trying to get in."

He moved silently forward and tried to turn the heavy iron handle without making it creak. Slowly opening the door until he could just squeeze his head through, he caught sight of a figure disappearing around a corner of the dark corridor.

"See anybody?"

"I think it was Aunt May."

———

THE BRIGHT WINTER'S SUN OF THE MORNING GAVE WAY TO A grey, heavy sky that enveloped everything within its grasp, dampening all noise into a dour quiet.

"Do you think we'll have a white Christmas?" Lyn slid her fingers into a pair of woollen gloves as she followed Ant around the frozen formal gardens of Stanton Hall.

"If you're saying the weather forecast predicts snow, then you can bet your last chocolate biscuit that the sun will crack the flags, plus we'll all be wearing shorts by Christmas day lunch." Ant adjusted his collar to protect his ears from a stiffening icy breeze.

Lyn looked to the heavens and received a solitary snowflake on the end of her nose for her troubles. "I don't know about that. It's cold enough and those clouds look as though they need to go on a diet."

Slowly making their way down the gravel pathway with an empty herbaceous border on one side and hard pruned rose bushes on the other, the sullen landscape looked as though it was collapsing into itself as if preparing for an onslaught of severe weather.

"You say the strangest of things, Lyn Blackthorn, clouds on a diet?"

She gave him one of her head teacher looks. "You're a philistine, Anthony Stanton. I was waxing lyrical if you must know." She playfully tugged on his arm.

Resisting Lyn's gesture to quicken the pace, Ant shook his head. "If you say so. Anyway, will you be seeing your parents over the holidays?"

Lyn let go of his arm and stuffed her gloved hands into her heavy coat. "Fortunately, Mum has gone to stay with her sister in Nottingham, while Dad has a taken off for a week in Spain with his new girlfriend. That means I don't have to spend my time as piggy in the middle listening to my long-divorced parents squabbling. Come to think of it, apart from Percy being missing, everything's coming up roses."

Ant held up a finger, then pointed to his left. "Everything except those, which need a good feed."

"What?" She turned and frowned.

"I was waxing lyrical. The roses, none there, feed them up."

Lyn wore a look of exasperation. "Don't give up the day job, that's all I have to say on the matter."

Several minutes passed as they wandered from one garden room to the next. Antony seemed happy to lose himself in the company of a woman he'd become much closer to since returning from active service.

"Anyway, never mind my parents, how do you think your mum and dad are doing. Gerald seems on excellent form."

Ant gently placed Lyn's hand in his. "You know *them*, neither want to admit the years are passing and they're not as mobile as they once were. One thing's for sure, they won't allow anyone to make a fuss. That reminds me, I hope Dr Thorndike gets here soon. Dad was serious when he said he needed his medication."

Lyn's smile faded as his words sank in. "Surely he keeps a small stock in case of emergency?"

"You'd think so, wouldn't you, but no chance. Dad maintains the National Health Service is strapped enough for cash without him and Mum hoarding tablets."

"Which means, if either of them runs out, they're in trouble?"

"Got it in one, Lyn."

Anthony bent down, picked up a frozen pebble and

threw it at a copper weathervane that sat on top of a dovecote.

"What are you doing, vandal?"

He picked up another pebble and handed it to her. "Don't sound so outraged. You were better at this than me when we were kids. Go on, give it your best shot."

Lyn took careful aim and let loose the stone. A few seconds later, the weathervane pinged and rotated through 180 degrees as her projectile found its target. "And I still am."

One of these days I'll beat you, Lyn Blackthorn.

Desperate to get himself out of his beaten corner, he turned to face the uneven façade of the Hall. "It's a lovely thing, isn't it?"

She brushed his cheek with a gentle kiss. "Is that your way of saying you surrender? Yes, it's wonderful, but I've never understood why it's so... well, knobbly."

He laughed. "I've heard Stanton Hall called may things, but never 'knobbly.' I presume you're referring to the bits and bobs added over the centuries. It's simple, really. When my ancestors had a bit of spare cash, they built an extension. In our case, cash came spasmodically, so you end up with a mishmash of mediaeval, Georgian and Victorian styles."

Lyn scanned the various architectural elements of the south wing. "Do you know, I've never noticed that before."

"Noticed what?"

She pointed to a corner junction between two parts of the house just below the roof line. "That tiny window. Why on earth would anybody put one there?"

Anthony peered through the dimming light to see what she was pointing at. "It's probably part of the servants' quarters. Like all big houses, they had small rooms in the roof spaces. Perhaps we should look sometime."

Lyn laughed. "Perhaps we should do it now; you never know, we might find your Uncle Percy up there."

He laughed. "I wouldn't put it past the man to have squirrelled himself away up—"

A voice cut through the chilled air.

"Sorry to disturb, sir. Your father has collapsed."

5

3:29 P.M. CHRISTMAS EVE

"What happened, Richard?"

The youngest member of the house staff still looked panicked as he shivered in the afternoon cold. "I was in the kitchen, sir, when his lordship's bedroom bell rang. By the time I got to his room, your father had collapsed. I spoke to the butler, and he said to fetch you straightaway."

A look of shock spread across Ant's face as the disturbing news sank in. "Thank you, Richard." He stood motionless for a few seconds.

I don't like the sound of this.

Lyn tugged at the crook of his arm. "Let's get going, not least for Richard here is shivering in his shirtsleeves." Her softly spoken words in an attempt at lightheartedness stirred her companion from his temporary melancholy.

As they neared the Hall entrance, the hubbub and sights of an excited family Christmas reunion cut through the chill atmosphere outside.

"Let's take the old female staff entrance to get up to Dad's bedroom. I don't want that lot to know what's going on. At least not yet."

Drifting to the left and rounding the front elevation of Stanton Hall, Richard led them through the redundant stable block and onto the dairy.

"I'd forgotten what a warren of buildings the Hall is," whispered Lyn as she continued to comfort her close friend.

With a deft click of the wooden doorknob and a sharp kick with the toe of his left foot to the bottom of this stubborn door, Richard gained entrance to a part of the building that its owners would've historically not concerned themselves with.

The trio entered a dark narrow passageway, which led to a narrow steep flight of stairs.

"Is there a light?"

"Sort of, sir." Richard felt for, and eventually found, a small bakelite switch mounted on a wooden block on the bare brick. "I'm sorry it's not brighter; shall I lead?"

Anthony looked up at the single light bulb dangling precariously in its socket from a spiderweb-strewn plaster ceiling full of holes.

"It's not your fault, Richard. You can put it down to my Victorian ancestors not being prepared to spend sufficient money on the comfort of its staff. Yes, if you wouldn't mind, lead on; I suspect you're more familiar with what's up there than I am."

Richard moved forward cautiously, wafting long-abandoned spiderwebs and other detritus to one side. "The handrail is a little temperamental, sir. I would ask you both to take great care."

Halfway up their ascent, a sharp crack broke an eerie silence. Anthony automatically gripped Lyn tighter to ensure her safety from a threat he couldn't make sense of.

"It's just a broken step, sir. Please be careful as you pass."

Twenty seconds later, all three found themselves clear of the creaking stairway and standing on a narrow landing.

"Imagine trudging up and down those things twenty times a day," said Lyn.

"It would've been all the worse before they installed electricity, however poor the result."

Opening a thin wood-panelled door which led on to a long, narrow passageway with a row of doors on its left, Richard again felt for a light switch and enabled a second light bulb to cast its dim shadow.

"Where are we?"

"The female staff living quarters, Lyn. Once we're through the door at the other end of the corridor, we'll be within twenty yards of Dad's bedroom."

As they stepped along the bare pine floorboards and passed several doors at approximately eight-foot intervals, the conditions in which servants had lived troubled Anthony.

Thank heavens those days have gone.

All three shielded their eyes as Richard led them through a two-sided door at the end of the corridor. On the servants' side, brown-painted wood panels cast a shadow along the already dark walls. In contrast, the other face enjoyed rich panelling that matched its sumptuous surroundings.

"It's called a jib door."

"What are you talking about, Ant?"

He pointed back at the door. "That's disguised to mimic its surroundings. It's called a jib door."

Lyn shook her head. "All smoke and mirrors then."

"That's quite a good way of summing up the old way of doing things." Anthony turned to Richard, thirty feet farther on, and stood at the earl's bedroom door.

"Come on, Ant, we've wasted enough time. Let's see how your father is."

He felt Lyn's hand as they walked side by side, unsure what he'd discover when Richard opened the bedroom door.

To his surprise, his father rested on top of the bed, leaning against an ornately carved oak headrest, his back supported by several billowing pillows.

The earl concentrated his look on Richard. "I said not to tell anyone, did I not?" The junior member of staff looked crestfallen. "Don't take it to heart, young man, I'm not criticising you. I'm sure you did exactly as David instructed." The elderly gentleman smiled as he kept eye contact with the man.

"And I should think so, too, Father. You're a rascal for frightening young Richard to death when he found you, then taking a pop at him for doing his job. He has yet to learn your rather strange sense of humour."

Ant watched as his father winked at the young man, who had begun to blush.

"And on that note, Richard, I think we should allow you to escape your awful employer to get on with whatever you were doing before he played the drama queen. Off you go. However, I would ask you to update the butler on what has happened. I want this kept from the family for as long as possible, yes?"

"Sir. If that will be all?" It was a question that required no response as the young man quietly walked to the bedroom door and quietly closed it behind him.

Lyn, who had moved forward to sit on the side of the earl's bed as the drama of the previous few minutes unfolded, patted the old man's hand as it rested on top of a sumptuous eiderdown. "You are a tease, Gerald. Fancy frightening that young lad half to death. And at Christmas too. Shame on you."

The earl returned Lyn's warm smile and winked.

"That's a habit your son has picked up from you, except he hasn't yet learned to use it as deftly as the Earl of Stanton."

Anthony felt himself blush as he stepped forward to sit next to Lyn on the edge of his father's bed. "We'll talk about that later, young lady. Right now, my father needs to explain what happened."

Both looked at the tired features of the old gentleman.

"I don't know. One of the more frustrating aspects of the passing years is that one can feel perfectly well. Then before you know it, you're on the floor looking up at the chandelier. Except this time, it was that silly lampshade that I've always hated."

He pointed to a brightly coloured shade with a crimson-stitched fringe.

Lyn glanced at a mahogany bedside table on which an empty pill box organiser rested. "When did you last take your medication, Gerald?"

The earl glanced at the opaque plastic box divided into seven sections, each marked with the day.

A moment's silence fell as the old man scratched his head. "If I'm being honest, my darling, I'm not sure."

Ant slapped a hand on the eiderdown in frustration. "You know what happens when you run out of your pills, Dad. Why did you leave it so late to call your new prescription in?"

He noticed Lyn's disapproving glare.

"Look, Dad," he now spoke in a more measured tone. "I'm sorry for—"

"There is no need to apologise, darling boy. Your father

is an old fool, but the doctor assured me he'd be over by lunchtime. I can't think what's happened to him, and I'm sure we have plenty of time."

As he finished speaking, the earl's eyes drooped, and in seconds, he was asleep.

Lyn put a finger to her lips. "Let's let him sleep," she whispered.

As they left the earl's bedroom Ant saw the butler walking towards them. "David, we have to find Dr Thorndike. I reckon we have three or four hours before the earl is in real trouble."

———

SOON, THE PAIR HAD DISCREETLY EXITED VIA A SIDE DOOR AND Anthony had fired up one of the estate's Land Rovers. "We'll try his surgery first and if he's not there, we track his receptionist down for a list of his house calls."

The journey into Stanton Parva passed without incident, and twenty-five minutes after setting off, Anthony slowed his vehicle to a stop outside the surgery of Dr Thorndike.

"It's not looking too promising, Lyn; I don't see any lights on." Leaping out of the driver's side, he hurried to the front door of the narrow building which sat in the middle of a row of thatch-roofed cottages.

"It's hardly surprising, is it? I guess most doctors would already be at home with the slippers on. We're lucky to have Dr Thorndike. Can you imagine any other doctor doing house calls on Christmas Eve?"

They stood side by side peering into the empty waiting room through a Georgian bow window.

"Nothing for it. We must head to his receptionist's place. Do you know where she lives?"

Before Lyn could respond, village gossips, Phyllis and Betty, were upon them. "You won't find him there, not today. It's Christmas Eve, you know," said Betty as she rearranged the hairnet over her recently permed purple locks.

Talk about stating the blindingly obvious.

"As you say, Phyllis. Not to worry, it was nothing urgent." Ant knew his casual aside wouldn't cut it with the redoubtable old lady.

"Is it your father, again? I can't think why you would be here if it wasn't important. Is he not feeling too well?"

Ant gave Lyn an impatient glance.

"As Lord Stanton says, nothing important. In fact, you may help." Lyn's request immediately sparked Phyllis' interest. "We just wanted to show our appreciation for all the hard work Dr Thorndike does for the village, and have a little gift for him. As you so rightly point out, he's not here. I wonder whether you might deliver a little gift when you see him next?"

Phyllis appeared delighted and chatted to Betty excitedly as Lyn stepped back to the Land Rover, opened the door and went inside.

"Oh dear."

"Is something the matter?" said Phyllis as she tried to see what Lyn was doing.

Stepping back from the Land Rover and closing the passenger door, Lyn met the villagers with a look of disappointment. "Would you believe it, in our haste to deliver several gifts, we seem to have forgotten to bring Dr Thorndike's."

Realising what Lyn was up to, Ant contributed to the charade. "My fault entirely, ladies, I'll give him a ring and apologise, although being the man he is, he won't expect anything. All the same, it's my mistake and I shall tell him so."

He caught Lyn smirking as he compounded her deception.

Phyllis and Betty looked at one another and shrugged their shoulders.

"Well, ladies, Lyn and I must be off; there is much to do up at the Hall, you know what it's like." He immediately realised he had made a mistake.

Phyllis pulled the collar of her fake fur coat around her ears. "Yes, Christmas is such a wonderful time, and folk can be so generous, especially to us older ones. I remember as children what happy times we had; I—"

"Except, dear, for that time when your father thumped the coal man for short-changing him on the number of bags he charged for. And then there was that time when—"

Phyllis bristled with indignation. "Yes, yes, never mind that now. You must always put a damper on things. I don't know why I bother with you."

Ant gave Phyllis a look of pity.

I don't know why you put up with that old battleaxe.

"Now, ladies, as you say, it's Christmas and we must be charitable to each other, don't you think?"

Oh dear, done it again.

Phyllis grasped her opportunity. "Are many villagers going to the Hall this evening for your traditional get together? We don't seem to have received invitations?"

He noticed Lyn stifling her laughter. "Quite a few, and I don't understand why you have not heard from us. You're most welcome to join us." Ant was sure he detected a look of triumph on Phyllis' face, while Betty seemed genuinely delighted.

"It will be wonderful to meet your family again, isn't that
so, Betty?"

The question was one which Phyllis neither expected
nor wanted her friend to reply to.

"I'm sure they haven't forgotten you, Phyllis."

Not after that fiasco with the punchbowl.

Finally free of Phyllis and Betty, the pair scoured each
cottage as they drove up the High Street looking for
number 112.

One tap on the solid wooden door, which featured one
tiny square pane of obscure glass high level, was enough to
alert the cottage's occupant.

"Goodness me, is everything all right? What on earth
brings you two here?"

Anthony explained the urgency of the situation, which
led the woman to scurry into the kitchen. Seconds later she
appeared holding a typed piece of paper. "The doctor
should have finished by now. He told me he had to give the
earl his medication. I don't understand what could have
happened to him, I just hope he hasn't had an emergency
during one of his calls."

Lyn held her hand out to the worried spinster. "I'm sure
everything's okay. We'll find him."

The woman pursed her lips as she looked at Lyn in
alarm. "It's just not like Dr Thorndike. He always rings if
there's a problem." Suddenly the woman's demeanour
improved. "That's it—I'll try his mobile. Just wait there."

As she ran down the narrow hallway to gather her
mobile phone, Ant shouted after her. "Listen, we'll start
checking the list you kindly gave us. You get through to him,
you have my number; please ring."

Without waiting for a reply, Ant urged Lyn to climb into
the Land Rover.

"Shouldn't we have waited?"

"Don't shout at me, Lyn. You know what the signal is like in the village, never mind out in the sticks. We must get going. If she gets through, that's fine, at least we'll already be on the way to meet him."

His explanation went some way to calm his passenger down. Minutes passed in silence as she tried to work out in which order they should visit Dr Thorndike's patients.

As time passed, Ant's anxiety increased. "That's four that he's been to and gone again. So it has to be the next one. How far away do you think we are?"

Lyn checked the address again. "Ten minutes, I reckon."

Her estimate proved correct as at last they stood at the front door of a solitary flint-faced cottage seemingly in the middle of nowhere. As Lyn rang the bell, snowflakes fell gently around them.

The opening door revealed a man of around thirty-five wearing the largest grin Ant had ever seen. "We're just looking for Dr Thorndike; I don't suppose he's still with you?"

"Come in, come in. What a beautiful Christmas Eve it turned out to be—and look—it's snowing."

The pair looked back over their shoulders to take in the wondrous scene as the man bodily pulled them into the petite lounge.

"I'm sorry, er, if Dr Thorndike isn't here, we really must get on. Do you know—"

"listen," the man pointed to the ceiling.

After a few seconds of silence, a baby's cry rang out.

"Come and say hello to Daisy. Our wonderful doctor delivered her. You must come up and have a look. My wife will want to show our daughter off to you."

Not waiting for an answer, the ebullient man was

halfway up the open staircase and looking back at the visitors to join him. Ant gave Lyn a desperate look.

"It'll take sixty seconds, that's all," she whispered.

He nodded almost imperceptibly. "Thank you so much"

Inside the pine-panelled bedroom, a tired-looking woman sat up in bed cradling her new child.

"Look who I brought to see us, Mavis."

His wife managed a friendly smile before returning her motherly gaze to her daughter.

After going through the pleasantries of peeking at the baby and congratulating the mother, Ant turned and whispered to the husband.

"The thing is, we must track Thorndike down; you see—"

"But I don't understand. The doctor told us he couldn't stay long after Daisy was born because he had to call in at Stanton Hall on an urgent matter." The man lifted his arm to look at his wristwatch. "He should have been there by now. I don't understand."

Ant shook his head. "Are you sure?"

The man looked at his wife and baby before turning back to his visitor. "Yes, he was clear he needed to get a move on, so I suggested he take one of the back roads that would've shortened his journey by nearly ten minutes."

"Would that be along Drovers Lane?" said Lyn.

"I know it twists and turns a bit, but nobody uses it much these days, I'm sure the doctor will be fine."

———

"THAT ROAD IS DANGEROUS THE BEST OF TIMES, THAT'S WHY nobody uses it. Take into consideration the ice still on the ground, and now this lot. I don't like it, Lyn."

The air was so cold and dry that he didn't need the Land Rover's windscreen wipers to clear away the snow.

Lyn rubbed the inside of the windscreen with tissues to clear the condensation from their line of view. "It's getting heavier, do you think Dr Thorndike's safe?"

Anthony was concentrating so hard on keeping the Land Rover away from the hopscotch of ice patches he didn't answer. He knew that in normal circumstances it would be harmless puddles.

As the minutes ticked by, the four-wheel-drive vehicle travelled deeper into Norfolk's snow-covered countryside as the heavy skies released a cascade of iced-white flakes.

We must move quicker.

Ant faced a dilemma in either driving prudently, considering the deteriorating weather, or getting back to the Hall where he hoped to meet Thorndike.

"Hold on, Lyn, I'm going to push it a bit. As long as no one is coming the other way, we'll be fine."

Lyn wrapped her left hand around the grab handle above her door and tried to stay supple, knowing that if they crashed, it might be better than tensing up. "You know I trust you. Just keep safe."

Ant leant forward towards the windscreen as if attempting to get nearer to the road surface. Ahead lay a blind bend that had caught several drivers out over the years.

"It's okay, Lyn, we'll be, oh no..."

As the Land Rover rounded the bend, he caught sight of a vehicle immediately ahead, a column of steam rising from its engine compartment.

"Watch out, we're going to hit it."

Keeping one hand on the steering wheel, he put the

other on the gearstick, while taking his foot off the accelerator and staying clear of the brake pedal. "I think..."

The Land Rover lost its grip as a tyre hit ice hidden
beneath the snow.

"Careful." Lyn looked across to him, her eyes beginning
to fill.

"Got it. Yes, got it." Ant returned both hands to the
steering wheel and allowed the Land Rover to drift off the
road and onto a narrow strip of snow-covered soil bordered
by a high hawthorn hedge. "Gently now, okay, into the
hedges we go."

As the Land Rover brushed the hedge, a cloud of snow
crystals flew in all directions as the friction of the timber
barrier brought the vehicle to a gentle stop. "Sorry about
that, hop out on my side."

Standing side by side in the blizzard-like conditions,
they peered through the deteriorating weather and the
appalling sight in front of them.

"It's a head-on crash. Heaven help us, I hope they're
okay."

Ant leant into the wind and moved forward.

"Is that the doctor's car?"

"I'm sure it is, Lyn. Come on, they'll need help."

Reaching the driver's door of Thorndike's car, Ant
smiled with relief seeing the doctor looking back at him.
Ant tried to open the door, but at first it wouldn't move.
Standing back and using the sole of one of his feet, he gave
the contraption a sharp kick.

"I've seen everything now," said Lyn as she stood in front
of her friend with her back to the ferocious wind to keep the
worst of the weather off them.

He pulled the door handle again. This time it moved.
"Oh ye of little faith."

Lyn tried her best to smile. "Is he okay?"

"I think so." Ant pulled harder at the door until it opened with a crunching sound that told him the chassis twisted in the accident.

"I'm fine, I'm fine, but we must see to that lady. I came around the corner. It was too late. She was, well, the car was just stopped there. I—"

"It's okay now, Dr Thorndike, you're safe. No need to explain, we almost hit you doing the same thing. Now, let's get you out."

Lyn had hurried back to the Land Rover and retrieved a large woollen blanket she found in the back seat. "Let's get this around you, Doctor, it'll warm you up."

Ant tried to help the man out of the car but stopped when the driver let out a yelp.

"My left foot is trapped by the clutch pedal. I don't know whether it's broken, don't pull. Can you look?"

Releasing his hold on the doctor, he bent forward to identify the problem. To Ant's relief, there didn't seem to be any major damage. "No problem. The pedal bent and caught the shoe. I'll have you out in a jiffy."

Lyn concentrated on making sure the blanket was covering as much of the doctor's head and torso as possible to shield him from the blizzard as her companion gently prised the damaged pedal away from Thorndike's foot.

"That's it, you're free. Let's get you out of here."

To everyone's surprise, Thorndike felt no pain as the two rescuers helped the man to his feet.

"I must get her."

Before they could answer, the doctor moved forward to walk around the rear of the car so he could get to the driver's side.

"She's unconscious. This woman's received treatment for

a head trauma. Perhaps she didn't wait long enough to recover from whatever injuries she suffered, and that's why I crashed into her."

Lyn caught up with Thorndike and continued to shield him from the blowing snow. "Never mind that now, Dr Thorndike; we'll call an ambulance."

Thorndike pressed two fingers to the injured woman's neck. "She has a strong pulse. It will be quicker for us to take her to the Hall, we can only be a few minutes away, rather than wait for an ambulance to make its way from Wroxham in this weather."

Lyn looked back at Ant who was making sure Thorndike's car ignition was off and that there was no danger of the battery causing a fire. "It's the doctor's call, but it makes sense to me. We can only be ten minutes or so away from Stanton Hall."

Both friends looked to the doctor for confirmation.

"She'll be a dead weight, but I think it's worth a try. I can assess her once we get back to the Hall and treat her appropriately."

Ant directed his attention to his mobile. "I'll give Fitch a ring for him to arrange recovery of the cars and alert the police to a danger in the road. Come on, let's get this sorted."

Getting the unconscious woman out of the car became hazardous as the wind blew the snow into drifts.

"Wait, I think she's..."

6

4:54 P.M. CHRISTMAS EVE

"Hold the lady there if you can. I'll pull the Land Rover up so we can get her into the front passenger seat." Driving snow continued to twist and turn as Anthony trod gingerly through the virgin snow, an angry wind propelling him forward.

Carefully manoeuvring his vehicle around the crash site, Ant opened his passenger door.

"We'll need a hand," shouted Lyn as the occupant of the car came around. "The quicker we can get moving, the better."

Lifting the lady out of her damaged vehicle and settling her into the Land Rover proved difficult. "We're getting in each other's way, Lyn. Dr Thorndike, can you just hold her head while I get her legs to swivel her around?"

The three companions each played their part as they eventually got the woman to her feet and guided her into the front seat of Ant's vehicle.

"Thank heavens for that," said Lyn as she squashed into the back seat with Dr Thorndike, and the Land Rover began its brief journey to Stanton Hall. Although the snowfall eased, Ant knew he couldn't relax for a second on the treacherous road.

Despite the urgency of the situation, Anthony marvelled at the winter scene that revealed itself as he gently coaxed the vehicle from one bend to another. Neat rows of plough lines protecting their precious winter crops lay hidden beneath a pristine sheet of white, which glistened in the Land Rover's headlights.

In the far distance, Bacton Woods pierced the flat landscape as if holding up the heavens.

"Dr Thorndike, are you okay?"

Ant looked over his shoulder to see Lyn gently nudging Thorndike, whose eyes were closed. "Anything the matter?"

Lyn squeezed the doctor's arm through his heavy winter coat. Still, there was no response.

"I think he's unconscious, we need to pull over."

As the Land Rover completed a controlled skid and came to a stop, the sideways movement of the vehicle caused Dr Thorndike to stir. "What? Have we arrived?"

Lyn squeezed the man's arm again. "Are you with us, Doctor? You had us worried for a few seconds."

Thorndike gave her a confused look, as if he didn't know what she was talking about.

"Are you sure we shouldn't take the woman to hospital. I know it will take us a month of Sundays to get there, but both of you have had a nasty shock."

Anthony kept eye contact with the medic via his rear-view mirror. He could also see the concern etched on Lyn's face. "What do you reckon?"

"I'm inclined to agree with you. If the doctor deteriorates, the authorities will want to know why we left two people to become ill, or, heaven help us, something even worse."

Up ahead, the road branched in two directions. Veering left would take them to Stanton Hall. Turning right set a course for the Norfolk and Norwich Hospital.

Five minutes to home, or at *least an hour to Norwich?*

He brought the vehicle to a stop several yards before the junction. "It's decision time, Lyn. Left or right?"

"Left. Left, I say." Dr Thorndike's voice was suddenly authoritative.

Anthony twisted around in his chair. "Are you sure, Doctor? As a medical professional, it will be you that the authorities go after if you make the wrong call."

A moment's silence followed as the two men fixed their unblinking gaze on each other. Dr Thorndike lifted his hand and pointed. "Left."

I hope you're right.

Releasing the handbrake and gently pressing on the accelerator, Anthony coaxed the old vehicle forwards.

Thank heavens for four-wheel drive.

Shortly after, they passed through a matching pair of mock-gothic gatehouses into the grounds of Stanton Hall.

"Two minutes and we'll be there," said Ant as he sighed with relief that they were off the main road.

To his left, his female passenger murmured.

Lyn tried to sit forward but her seatbelt wouldn't allow it "What's she saying, Ant?"

He leant to his left, trying to catch the woman's words over the noisy diesel engine of the Land Rover.

The woman repeated a single word.

"I think she said, Nick?"

"Nick? Do you think she wants us to contact someone for her, perhaps family?

The woman repeated herself.

"It's definitely, Nick. You're right, Lyn, she must want us

to get in touch with whoever he or she is. Let's get inside and we can sort it all out."

What a Christmas this is turning out to be.

———

"And just how are we going to get this lady into a bedroom without the rest of your family thinking we've kidnapped her?" Lyn propped the woman up with one hand while holding the Land Rover door open with another to avoid it flying loose in the strengthening wind.

Anthony smiled. "I have a cunning plan."

Lyn looked horrified. "If you think I'm lugging this one up those stairs that almost collapsed on us, you've another thing coming, sunshine."

"Don't be so silly, would I do that to you?"

"Do you really want me to answer that, Anthony Stanton?" Her expression left him in no doubt of the low esteem she held him in.

"Despite your lack of confidence in my ability to squirrel this one upstairs pronto, you must wait one minute, then I shall reveal all."

Before Lyn could question him further, he made off through a darkened entrance of the Hall to reappear shortly, carrying a collapsed wheelchair.

As Dr Thorndike, now sat in the driver's seat, attended to his patient, Lyn looked on in amazement as Anthony shuffled his way through a four-inch covering of snow.

"Better you than me trying to push her in that thing. Are you sure it works?"

Lifting his chin slightly to show an air of indifference, Anthony lowered the contraption to the floor and prised open the handles.

Thank goodness it's all here.

"On your head, be it. Ten quid you tip her into the snow."

"You're on," replied Ant as he positioned the chair next to the open passenger door of the Land Rover.

It took several attempts to get the semiconscious woman safely into the wheelchair; Anthony lost no time getting everyone across the stable yard and into an old tack room.

"I have no wish to be a killjoy, Anthony, but how do you suggest we get this lady onto the first floor and into a bedroom?"

Lyn piled in." Excellent question, Dr Thorndike. And the answer is…?"

Ant now played his trick card. "If my memory serves me right, there is an old service lift down the service corridor. We can chuck her in there and whip her upstairs."

The doctor looked horrified. "You mean to—"

"Ah, I apologise Dr Thorndike; I didn't mean, literally chuck the woman. There should be enough room for the wheelchair and one of us." He looked at Lyn.

She shook her head. "You must be joking. I doubt you've any idea that it works. In fact, I doubt you know when the thing was last used. What on earth makes you think I'm prepared to trap myself in an iron cage while you press the button and send us shooting through the roof, wheelchair and all?"

The doctor sympathised with Lyn. "I think Miss Blackthorn makes a rather good point, don't you? However, whatever you do, I think we need to get a move on. This lady is getting colder, as am I, and then there's your father to see to."

Thorndike's common-sense approach dragged Anthony back to reality. "You're right, Doctor, and I'm sorry for teasing you Lyn. Cards on the table. Jimmy, a long-standing member of the team, told me about the lift a few months ago and showed me the thing. So I know it works. Come on, get going."

He sensed he should avoid looking at Lyn as he glanced at her white knuckles on a handle of the wheelchair.

Within seconds, a marvel to Victorian invention revealed its secrets.

"And what exactly is that big handle for?"

Anthony stepped over to the contraption and patted the cast-iron construction. "They installed it before the days of electricity, or at least before the family was prepared to extend it to the working side of the house. In you go." He pulled back the steel latticed gate, which caused a cloud of dust to descend from the ceiling.

"Don't look so sceptical, Lyn Blackthorn, it's safe. You get in, I close the door and turn this handle and off you go."

Lyn wheeled the chair into the small space and gave Anthony a venomous look. "They say what goes up must come down. If that happens to me, your life would not be worth living. Do I make myself understood?"

I hope Jimmy fixed the brake.

"Nothing at all to worry about, it has quite a sophisticated safety system. If anything goes wrong an emergency brake will cut in and stop you disappearing through the floor. Now, hang on."

"Wait a second, you said, *if*?"

Anthony ignored the comment and began furiously winding a handle attached to the iron wheel.

Good heavens, it works.

"Didn't I tell you there was nothing at all to worry about? Just one thing, you need to tell me when your feet are at the same level as the landing. Just so I know when to stop turning."

The voice from above displayed a great deal of displeasure. "When my feet... I'll give you feet. Just wait until I get hold of you."

Dr Thorndike raised an eyebrow to Anthony.

"It's okay, Doctor, she'll soon calm down. At least I hope she does," whispered Anthony as he continued to turn the handle at speed. The higher the lift went, the greater the volume of metal grinding against metal became.

"Now, now. Stop this stupid thing now."

What Ant hadn't realised was that the inertia of the drive wheel took a few seconds to diminish, meaning that Lyn's feet now stood several inches above the landing floor level.

"And how do I get this poor lady out of here? Shall I push off the edge and see what happens, or ask her to abseil to the landing floor?"

The doctor shook his head in despair as Anthony pondered his next action.

And it was going so well.

"Don't worry, I'll turn the handle the other way."

Never done this bit.

Attempting to hide his nervousness from Thorndike, Anthony pivoted a handle on the gear assembly until it clumped into place with a heavy thump. Tentatively, he turned the big wheel anticlockwise. To his delight, he could see the lift beginning to descend.

"That's it, stop, now."

He didn't need telling twice and immediately stopped turning and locked off the mechanism. "Told you there wouldn't be a problem." He winked at the doctor who seemed to be in a world of his own.

A few minutes passed as Anthony brought the lift down to ground level.

"In you get, both of you. I'll show you how it's done." Lyn turned the handle of the first-floor mechanism, which mirrored the one Anthony had used.

I knew she'd be better at it than me.

———

DR THORNDIKE TIDIED THE BEDCLOTHES OVER HIS PATIENT and stood back to observe how she looked. "I've examined the woman and confident she will be fine. Whoever attended to her did an excellent job on that head wound."

Lyn looked at her surroundings. "I don't suppose it's every day you get to rest in a genuine mediaeval four-poster bed, so I hope she enjoys it."

Thorndike gave her a sideways glance. "I suspect the lady would rather be in her own bed, wherever that might be, don't you?"

A bit sharp. Maybe the accident was worse than you say?

Anthony glanced at Lyn. "It's okay," she whispered.

Behind them, a door opened into the exquisitely wood-panelled bedchamber.

"Thank you for popping up, Maisie. Perhaps you could stay with this lady for a while to make sure she remains comfortable, and to alert me if the need arises?"

"Sir," responded Maisie as she quietly stepped over to the bed and sat on an old oak chair next to her sleeping charge.

———

"I DON'T THINK YOUR NEXT PATIENT WILL BE SO COMPLIANT, DR Thorndike. However, you've known my father long enough to see through his little tricks."

Thorndike rubbed his forehead as they walked along a grand corridor towards the earl's bedroom.

"Are you sure you feel okay, Doctor?" Lyn's voice carried an overt tone of concern.

They were already at the earl's door before Thorndike thought to answer. Tapping gently on the ornately decorated entrance, Anthony quietly opened the door allowing all three to step inside.

"He's well away," commented Lyn as she looked on the earl sleeping peacefully in his immense bed.

Thorndike approached and felt the earl's pulse. After what seemed like an age, he stepped back. "Your father's pulse is steady, and he's only due his medication at six, so I propose to let him sleep until then."

Contented that a professional had judged his father safe to leave for the time being, Anthony sighed. "Well, that's a relief, Doctor. Thank you for all you've done this afternoon, I know it's been a testing time for you and I'm not fully convinced that you escaped that awful crash unscathed."

Thorndike brushed Ant's concerns aside. "Not at all, all in a day's work. However, I would appreciate a drink of something, if I may?"

Ant laughed quietly so as not to disturb his father. "I agree, let's get you settled into the library so you can have a bit of peace away from the madness that is my family at Christmas."

Lyn caught Ant's attention as Thorndike steadied himself on the door frame of the bedroom door as he exited the landing. "He's not himself," she whispered.

"I agree, Lyn, all the more reason to get him in a quiet space."

They took the time to guide Thorndike down a set of service stairs before reappearing into a ground floor corridor which, amongst other rooms, led to the library. Inside, a roaring fire glowed in a marble fireplace, throwing dancing shadows onto the bookshelves.

"Let's get you settled here." Lyn guided Thorndike into a red leather wingback chair next to the fireplace.

The doctor relaxed and gazed into the flames. In seconds, he fell asleep.

"Let's give the man some peace, Ant, we can look in on him in half an hour."

———

LYN STOOD IN FRONT OF ONE OF THE LARGE GLASS PANELS OF the conservatory and looked out on the snow-covered grounds of Stanton Hall. "Don't the Christmas trees look marvellous with all those lights twinkling?"

Anthony wandered up to stand behind her and placed a hand on her shoulder. "It's beautiful, isn't it, and to top it all we have snow." He placed a gentle kiss on her cheek before stepping back and turning towards a small silver tray resting on a mahogany coffee table.

"Drink?"

Lyn turned around and smiled at him. "Is it eggnog?"

He laughed. "What do you expect on Christmas Eve?"

Half filling two glasses, he handed one to Lyn. "Here's to finding Uncle Percy safe and well."

Mention of his missing uncle's name caused both to fall into a thoughtful silence. The only sound came from the distant hubbub of the Stanton family revving itself up for the festivities to come.

"I tell you what, why don't we nip down to the kitchens and see what Mrs Smithson has got for us. It's something I used to do every year when I was a child."

Lyn smiled as he led the way back down the corridor, through a service door and down into the extensive range of kitchens that once served the Hall. Walking through a brick archway into the stone-floored preparation area, they both wore Cheshire Cat-like grins.

"Mrs Smithson, I—"Anthony's smile disappeared in an instant as he caught sight of the cook's state of distress. "What on earth's the matter?"

When Mrs Smithson caught sight of the earl's son, she tried her best to compose herself. "Oh, I'm just being silly, that's all."

Lyn stepped forward and gave her a hug. "Come on, tell me what's been going on. This isn't like you at all."

The cook retrieved a paper tissue from her apron and sat down on the pine chair with her elbow on the corner of a large table. "There's so much to do and I'm worried your meal won't be ready in time. I've never let the family down before and have no intention of doing so today."

Anthony dragged a chair over the stone floor causing it to sound like chalk scratching a blackboard and sat next to Mrs Smithson. "What can we do to help?"

The cook filled up again and began tapping two fingers on the tabletop. "If I'm being truthful, Mr Anthony, you can stop some members of your family waltzing in and out of my kitchen asking daft silly questions. How do I know what happened to your Uncle Percy? And what has it got to do with me that Cedric threatened your Aunt May. Do they think I'm an eavesdropping gossip who knows everything that goes on at the Hall?"

Wow, they've really got to you this time.

He looked to Lyn for support.

"Well, Mrs Smithson, we'll soon put a stop to this nonsense. You just leave it to Anthony and me. There will be no more interruptions." Just then, the sound of footsteps filled the air.

"Here we go again," said the cook, using the tissue to blow her nose.

Anthony immediately sprang to his feet just about to stop whoever it was coming in when he realised it was a footman holding a silver tray on which sat afternoon tea for one.

"Sir, I have just tried to deliver refreshments to Dr Thorndike in the library. However, sir, the gentleman had left the room. Do you know where I might find him?"

Lyn was standing at a large window, which allowed light to flood into the preparation area. "I know where he is."

Anthony turned from the footman towards his companion. "What are you talking about?"

She pointed at the walled garden, which stood fifty feet from the kitchen.

He rushed to the window and peered out onto the snow-covered scene. "Good heavens, we have to get after him. If he has another funny turn and gets lost out there, the cold will kill him."

Lyn grabbed hold of Anthony's arm. "There's not only the doctor to think about. If he goes missing, there's no one to medicate your father. By my reckoning, there's less than an hour before he needs treating."

The pair hurried out of the rear door to see Thorndike disappearing into the tree line.

"If he gets too far in there, we'll never find him," shouted Ant as he attempted to make himself heard above the howling wind.

By the time they reached the trees there was no sign of the doctor.

"At least we got shelter from that bitter wind," said Lyn

as she stood shivering in the shadow of a thousand trees. Both had run from the kitchen without giving the weather a second thought.

"Here, put this on. No arguing." Anthony took off his woollen jumper and handed it to Lyn.

She quickly slipped the garment overhead and rubbed her hands together.

As they considered whether to stay together or split up in the search for the doctor, the sound of a man crying in pain ricocheted off the densely packed tree trunks.

"That'll be Thorndike. He must have slipped. Where the heck is he?" Anthony brought the side of his fist down on a tree in frustration.

A second cry of pain rang out.

"Over there, I reckon," shouted Lyn as she set off toward the anguished sound.

It didn't take long for them to track Thorndike down. Although virtually no snow had penetrated the dense canopy, there was enough to follow footprints.

"What are you up to, Dr Thorndike?" Anthony tried to keep calm but knew the doctor and his father were both in danger.

Thorndike looked up from his slumped position against a tree trunk, tears in his eyes. "It's your father. I left his medication in the car when you rescued me. It's unforgivable. I must get back to my car, there is so little time. I'm so sorry." Within seconds, Thorndike had completely broken down.

Lyn knelt in the thin covering of powdery snow and gave what comfort she could.

"I'll try the mobile and see if I can get help."

This will never work.

He made three attempts to get through to the Hall; each

time the signal dropped out. "Lyn, we're on our own. I need you to get the doctor back indoors while I go back to the crash site. It will be quicker for me to go cross-country than bother with the Land Rover. Let's just hope his car hasn't been towed away yet. I don't even want to think about the consequences of that happening."

7

5:26 P.M. CHRISTMAS EVE

G uiding an agitated professional worried about his patient back to the Hall proved to be a challenging task for Lyn.

"Dr Thorndike, if you don't help me, you'll end up with frostbite and be in no position to help the earl. Do I make myself clear?"

The doctor eventually acknowledged his rescuer and cooperated with her efforts to get him indoors. With no choice but to take him through the main entrance of the ancient building, she knew it would be impossible to get him upstairs without someone noticing.

Fortunately, the butler, David, had his wits about him as he opened the heavy entrance doors. "May I help madam with the gentleman? perhaps the Christmas spirit has arrived a little early."

Several heads turned to catch sight of the visitor, his coat still sparkled white with snow from his stumble in the woods. Lyn immediately understood what the butler was up to.

Time for a little role play.

"A little too much of his home-made mulled wine. I warned him, he makes it far too strong every year."

None of the family recognised Lyn, or the doctor, as David whispered that she should keep her head down, while he took control of Thorndike.

"Perhaps your husband may benefit from a quick nap. Perhaps you might follow me to a guestroom."

Lyn followed David as he crossed the hallway and began ascending the grand staircase, holding Thorndike tight against his side.

"Thank you for your kindness, which my husband does not deserve. I agree we should get him to bed." Lyn placed an arm around her make-believe husband to help David get the man upstairs.

Lyn settled Thorndike into a high-backed upholstered chair in one of the smaller bedrooms on the first floor, kept cosily warm by two hot water radiators and a three-bar electric fire.

"Please stay here, Dr Thorndike, and warm yourself up. David will arrange for some food and a hot drink. Please don't worry about the earl. Anthony will be back before you finish your meal, so you can medicate his father. Do you understand?"

Thorndike raised his head to look at Lyn and nodded.

She turned to the butler. "Please keep an eye on him, David. You'll appreciate how important it is we don't lose him again."

"Of course, madam, I shall arrange everything."

As Lyn opened the door to leave the room, she turned back to David. "I don't suppose you've seen Mr Cedric, have you?"

"The last time I saw the gentleman, he was about to enter the armoury, madam," responded David.

Cedric wants the armoury, I wonder?

To avoid crossing the entrance hall again, Lyn repeated the route Ant had used earlier. She purposely opened the door to the armoury without knocking. Her scheme worked.

"Oh, I'm sorry, I didn't realise anyone would be in here."

I suppose a little fib is okay.

Cedric almost jumped from his wooden stool as his uninvited guest launched herself into the small space. "Goodness me, you're going to give an elderly man a heart attack." Cedric placed both hands across the centre of his chest to emphasise the point.

Lyn smiled sweetly. "I'm sorry, Cedric, I'm sure you know that isn't my intention. Not least, you're one of my favourites."

Cedric smiled. "Only *one* of your favourites?"

She approached the untidy table and planted a delicate kiss on the forehead. "Does that tell you anything?"

Flattery never hurts.

Cedric blushed. "I suppose I might forgive you on this occasion. Now, how can I help you?" He leant back a little too far, and almost fell backwards.

"Oops, do be careful, a heart attack is one thing, a broken neck will require a great deal more explanation to the police." Lyn leant forward to steady the old gentleman.

"Police? Who said anything about the police?"

What an odd reaction.

Lyn smiled as she straightened Cedric's tie. "You know, unexplained death and all that... Ah, sorry. I forgot about Percy. Unforgivable of me, I'll leave you to it."

That was crass of me.

Cedric composed himself and rearranged several of the old parchments spread out in front of him. "Not at all, my dear. I'm sure my brother can quite take care of himself. To be honest, I needed time away from Anthony's Aunt May. She drives me crazy. "So, one set of old bones reading about even older bones from the family archives offered a good alternative."

Lyn seized her opportunity. "It's sometimes better, Cedric, to talk about things, don't you think?"

The elderly man toyed with a red silk ribbon attached to a large white seal on one parchment. "My family does not differ from any other, Lyn. Sometimes we argue about incidents that happened so long ago, but no one can remember what exactly happened. Rather stupid, don't you think?"

"I know the longer a disagreement festers, the worse it gets and becomes harder to fix. In my experience, it's easier not to bother trying to resolve matters."

Cedric carefully pushed several parchments forward, so he could lean on his elbows. "That's the point, Lyn; May does not believe me when I say I don't understand why he did it."

Lyn lowered herself onto her haunches, so she was level with her companion. "The wedding?"

He hesitated before answering, gave a heavy sigh and folded his arms across his chest. "Percy stormed into the church just as the wedding vows were being said. He blurted out that to continue with the service would be illegal. In an instant, the groom ran from the church and, as far as I know, was never seen again. And before you ask, the matter was off limits after that. If May knows the real reason, I assume she will take it to her grave."

"Yet she thinks you assisted your brother in whatever drove him to intervene that day?"

Cedric uncrossed his arms and turned on his stool to face Lyn. "Percy has never explained. However, May won't have it."

Lyn took hold of his hand. "I'm so sorry. I know what it's like when there's tension within the family. Unfortunately, common sense seems to go out the window sometimes, doesn't it? There was no one else?"

Cedric shook his head. "As far as I know, she showed no interest after that. It wasn't for the lack of offers, I can tell you, she was quite a catch."

Time to change the subject, I think.

"The other great mystery concerns what happened to your brother."

Cedric withdrew his hand from hers and tensed. "As I've said, this is not the first time Percy has taken off and I doubt it shall be the last. He could be anywhere, but I tell you this: it would be something to do with the Hall's history; he's obsessed with the place."

Lyn smiled. "Well, he is a professor of history."

Cedric tapped the table with his index finger. "Yes, but it goes well beyond that. It's as if he's trying to right some great wrong. Except for when he wants something, he excludes us."

"What do you mean?" Lyn could see Cedric was becoming agitated.

"Take yesterday, for example. Percy sent me on a wild-goose chase to a National Trust property: Baddesley Clinton Manor House, except it was closed."

Lyn shrugged her shoulders. "Why did he send you?"

Cedric banged the table, which made Lyn jump. "That's the point, my dear. My brother talks in riddles, he said to ask them about the scullery. I ask you; he gave me no context, nor why he was so interested in only that room. He drives me mad."

"Mad enough to harm him, Cedric?" Lyn regretted her outburst immediately.

What have I done?

Cedric gave Lyn a cold, hard stare. "How dare you."

———

SHAKEN FROM CEDRIC'S POINTED WORDS AND RAPID departure from the armoury, Lyn took a moment to gather her thoughts.

I didn't expect that.

She glanced at the jumble of parchments in front of her.

What was he looking for when I came in?

After several minutes moving from one parchment to the next trying to discover what might have caught the man's interest, Lyn gave up.

This is a waste of time, let's see what May says.

Resolving not to make the same mistake twice in the space of a few minutes, Lyn knew she mustn't raise the question of the old lady's past. Following a hunch, she returned to the long gallery.

As she stood in the half-open doorway, Lyn noticed May watching a group of children at the far end of the ample room.

Before she could say hello, May caught sight of her. "Children, rather pointless little creatures, don't you think?" She patted the seat next to her to show where Lyn should sit.

Ambling over, Lyn smiled and playfully wagged a finger at May. "That's the second time in as many hours you have disparaged the future generation. You can't really expect me to agree with you, Lady Epping?"

Lyn took a seat without breaking eye contact with Anthony's formidable aunt.

May picked up her needlework. "And you can forget that

nonsense. I have a title only because a long-dead knight did the king's bidding and was rewarded for doing so. I have neither earned it nor a particularly desire to use it. Take this place"—she waved a hand around the oak-panelled space —"all won on the turn of a card, which also allowed them to call themselves earls and lord it over everyone else. Utterly ridiculous, don't you think? Call a spade a spade, that's what I say."

Now that's a surprise. Perhaps there's a soft centre under that granite shell.

"I agree, May. So, if we carry on in that vein, have you any idea what has happened to Percy?"

This will go one of two ways.

May rolled her eyes and sighed. "Always the same, that one. Percy thinks the world revolves around him and his ivory towers at Oxford University. He's never grown up, that's his trouble."

Suddenly a child's scream penetrated the enormous space. Lyn looked around to see a round wooden shield rolling across the oak floorboards, having fallen from the wall.

In an instant, she was up and hurrying towards the children while May continued with her needlework. Reassuring the group that they were safe, she suggested finding and asking the butler if they might pick a chocolate from one of the Christmas trees. Within seconds, the youngsters skipped down the long gallery in excited anticipation of their reward for being brave.

Lyn picked up the heavy shield and was about to rehang it when she noticed two overlapping "V" marks that the shield had hidden. Lyn recognised them as Witch Marks.

"It's said that they represent the Virgin Mary's initials as an invocation to protect the room, and anyone in it, from evil. Apt for Christmas Eve, don't you think?"

It took Lyn a few seconds to recover from the shock of discovering May standing behind her. "Then let's hope they offer Percy some protection."

"It will take more than a few scratches on the wall to do that, Miss Blackthorn."

————

As Lyn descended the grand staircase, she heard a loud banging coming from the front door. Before she could get there, David was opening the weighty structure.

Outside stood the bedraggled figure of a man dressed in a tattered coat, long woollen scarf and a grubby fedora hat. Windblown snow swirled around the strange figure, giving him an almost ethereal look.

Lyn made for the door, hoping the solitary figure was Percy. It soon became apparent this was not the case.

The man fell forward. It took all Lyn and David's strength to gather him up.

"We are a home for waifs and strays now, are we?"

A woman's voice from the landing above boomed around the voluminous space. "Behave yourself, Michael. Remember where you came from. Show some humility or get out."

Lyn looked up to see May pointing at the man who immediately vacated the hallway.

The two women shared a smile before Lyn redirected her attention to the newcomer, she could see he was half unconscious." Sit him on this chair, David, let's at least try making him comfortable."

The butler unbuttoned the bedraggled man's heavy coat,

which revealed an equally shabby cardigan and checked shirt.

The man's eyes darted between his two helpers as Lyn took hold of his hand. "He's freezing, David. We need to warm him up. Do you think you can find him some clean clothes and get him fed?"

The mention of food instantly attracted the man's attention. He sat up in his chair, his eyes burning into David.

"Of course." This time the stranger cooperated, and it only took the butler to get him on the move.

As they passed a small half-round, marble-topped table next to the entrance to the dining room, Lyn noticed the new arrival pocket a small silver crucifix and chain, which rested elegantly over a simple oak display stand. She decided against saying anything.

She turned to close the heavy front door against the inclement weather Ant saw the blue flashing light of a police car racing towards her.

Seconds later she watched as Ant rushed from the vehicle and ran toward her. "Ah, the second stranger in as many minutes. Have you got them?" Lyn's smile vanished as she watched Anthony lower his gaze to the floor.

"Thorndike's car has gone, and with it, his medication. Heaven help my father."

8

5:49 P.M. CHRISTMAS EVE

" W here is he?"

"Upstairs. Come on, I'll take you to him."

Anthony sped forward, leaving Lyn in his wake. In seconds he was hurtling along a landing corridor before he realised Lyn hadn't told him which room Dr Thorndike was in.

"Calm down, running around the place like a madman will solve nothing. He's in here." She stopped ten feet from where he was standing and pointed to a door. "Are you coming?"

He knew Lyn was talking sense and breathed more slowly as he followed her into the small bedroom. Dr Thorndike was sitting where Lyn had left him, except he was fast asleep.

"If you haven't got his bag, I can't see any point in waking him now, can you?" whispered Lyn.

Ant nodded. "It's such a mess," he replied in a hushed tone. "When I got to the crash site, Fitch's mate had beat me to it, recovered both cars, and with them went Dad's medication.

"Fortunately, the police were still making the road safe and agreed to radio for a patrol car to head to the pound. Hopefully, they'll get the medicine here in time."

Lyn gestured for him to follow her out of the bedroom and quietly closed the door behind. "What a day this is turning out to be. "

Anthony raised his eyes to the ceiling. "Somewhat of an understatement, I think. Anyway, how have you been getting on with my crazy family?"

Lyn briefed him on events while he was out. "But besides all that, we still have Percy to find. Given he's injured, I'm amazed the police haven't found his car, let alone him."

"And I thought I'd had it tough. At least you seem to have made friends with May, and that takes some doing. You don't think one of the family is responsible for Percy, do you? I know some of them are crazy, but I can't see any of them resorting to violence."

Lyn took hold of Ant's hand as they sauntered along the corridor until they reached the earl's bedroom. "I've experienced a few flashes of temper from your lot over the last hour. The logical side of my brain tells me it's ridiculous to think like that. Then again, as Peter Riley will tell you, most victims know the murderer."

"Murder? Who said anything about murder?"

Lyn squeezed his hand." How many times have we investigated a crime scene only to discover someone close to the dead person was responsible? Why should your lot be any different? Think about it, a man disappears into thin air, we find a large pool of blood where he was staying and your family act like a nest of vipers."

Anthony stopped in his tracks.

Perhaps Lyn's right. What if one of them killed Percy?

"I agree that something is wrong and the longer this goes

on without finding Percy makes the situation even more dangerous for him. Murder?"

"All I'm saying, Ant, is don't close your mind to anything. You taught me that. Wouldn't it be dreadful if we saved your father's life, only to lose another member of your family?"

What would I do without you, Lyn?

"Well, I've had two of my father's forestry staff scouring the whole estate for hours. So far, nothing. Yes, Percy's car has definitely gone because one thing is certain, it isn't anywhere on our land."

Lyn quietly turned the door handle to the earl's bedroom door. Opening it just far enough to peek in, she turned back to Anthony and smiled. "He's snoring like the old soldier he is."

Thank heavens for that.

"Well, that's one less thing to worry about, at least for now. Though Thorndike is correct, things will deteriorate quickly from here on in if he doesn't get his medication."

Lyn quietly closed the bedroom door and gestured for them to make their way downstairs. "Any news on Inspector Riley?"

Anthony stiffened. "That's another thing. His colleagues tell me the hospital wanted to keep him in for observation. In any event, the man discharged himself. Which means we—"

"Oh no, his dog. We said we'd look after it and it went clean out of my head with everything else going on. Shouldn't we get round to his place and bring it back here?"

"Its more likely Peter is at home himself now and gorging the thing on doggy Christmas treats."

Lyn shook her head. "Do we want to take the chance? Anyway, if we find Peter there, at least we know he's safe."

Logical, as usual.

"Which means you're going to send me out in this weather again, are you?"

She clung onto his arm as they reached the bottom of the impressive staircase. "Except this time, you'll have me for company. Anything to get away from your lot for half an hour."

"Whoopee-doo."

"I'll whoopee-doo, you, Anthony Stanton. Just for that, I'll drive the Land Rover."

He looked horrified. "You must be joking, I'll—"

"Ah, there you are, sir"—the butler interrupted his employer's flow—"I just wanted to check if, given the weather and certain family events, tonight's celebration will take place as planned?"

Anthony looked at Lyn, then back at the butler. "David, unless you're prepared to risk the village rising in rebellion, we carry on. And remember, no one outside the family is to know anything is wrong. The villagers expect their usual Christmas Eve party with all the usual bells and whistles, and that is what they shall have."

———

"FOR GOODNESS' SAKE, LYN, WILL YOU PLEASE SLOW DOWN. I know it's stopped snowing but look at the roads." Anthony looked across at Lyn while pinning his right arm to his side to stop himself grabbing the steering wheel.

"You don't like it when the boot is on the other foot, do you? I'm not driving any different to you earlier on. Your problem is that you always like to be in control. This time, I am—so be quiet, and grab hold of that handle." She pointed to the grip above the passenger door she'd been forced to use when he was driving.

Despite the treacherous road conditions, the Land Rover made light work of the snow-covered tarmac as Lyn brought the vehicle to a stop outside Detective Inspector Peter Riley's isolated cottage.

Walking carefully up a narrow pathway that led to the front of the cottage, a dog's bark penetrated the otherwise stillness of the early evening.

"Can you see anything?" Asked Lyn as her companion peered through the glass of a large bay window next to the front door.

"It's not in the lounge. In fact, the whole place looks in darkness. Let's try around the back."

Holding on to each other to avoid slipping as they navigated a snowdrift that had piled against the side of Riley's house, the inevitable happened.

"Hang on to me," laughed Anthony as he lost his grip and pulled Lyn over with him."

"You're a daft lump," squealed Lyn as she toppled on top of him, both now gazing at one another, inches apart.

Unable to move, they broke out into a fit of giggles.

"That was your fault," said Anthony as he cleared a space around their heads from the stable snowdrift.

"Rubbish, call yourself an intelligence officer, do you? An officer you may be, as for the other bit..."

She rested the side of her head on his upper chest, which was rising and falling at speed because of the amount of laughing he was doing.

"You intend lying there all night."

Anthony thought for a moment. "Two things occur to me. The first is that I can't get up until you move. It's not that you're overweight or anything, you're just pinning me onto a freezing layer of snow."

"You almost dug yourself into a hole, Anthony Stanton. What's the second thing, anyway?"

"I'm not going anywhere until you give me a kiss."

Lyn laughed as she raised her head from his chest. She wore a beaming smile. "That's blackmail!"

He shook his head, causing snow from the drift to penetrate both ears.

"Yuck."

"I hope you're not referring to me, Lord Red Nose."

He mirrored her smile. "You call it blackmail, I see it as opportunism. Anyway, your choice."

Lyn sighed. "Well, I've no intention of lying in the snow for the next few hours, so I suppose I'd better get it over with."

"You cheeky—"

Anthony didn't have time to finish his sentence before Lyn closed her lips onto his. A split second later, Peter Riley's dog barked again.

"Do you think his springer spaniel is prudish?"

"I don't know about that, Lyn, but you can tell she belongs to a police officer. They always spoil the fun."

The pair broke into laughter again as Anthony rolled them to the side, allowing both to scramble to their feet.

Lifting a latch on the back gate, he pushed hard, which turned the wooden gate into a snow plough as it cleared a path to open. Shuffling into the back garden, they made their way to a set of patio doors.

"There she is," said Lyn.

The animal stopped barking and instead gave the two visitors a curious look as she cranked her head to one side as if trying to solve a puzzle.

"One thing's for certain, Peter isn't here, which begs the

question where the silly man went when he discharged himself from hospital."

Her companion trod carefully over to the back door. "We haven't got time to ponder that one at the moment, Lyn."

I wonder?

"What are you doing?"

Anthony tilted the concrete birdbath over a few inches and felt beneath its base. A few seconds later he stood up and proudly held the key between two snow-dusted fingers. "You really would think the police officer would know better, wouldn't you?"

In seconds, the door was open as Lyn lifted the animal under her arm.

"She doesn't seem the least bit bothered we have kidnapped her, does she?"

Lyn ruffled the dog's hair and kissed her forehead.

"That's because Aunt Lyn is going to give her lots of cuddles."

He shook his head in disbelief. "I tell you what, I'll give the police station a ring to find out if he went there." Walking through the kitchen into the narrow vestibule, Anthony picked up the handset of an old-fashioned telephone from a narrow table at the bottom of the stairs.

Thirty seconds passed as he attempted to make contact. "All the lines must be dead, Lyn. I'll try my mobile."

Lyn busied herself keeping the dog amused.

"Nope, it's no good, we're on our own. Let's get going."

He led the way out of the house, locked the door and placed the key back in its secret place.

"Here, you take her" said Lyn as she thrust the springer spaniel into Anthony's unwilling arms.

"What?"

Lyn laughed. "You know precisely what it means. I drive;

you doggy sit. You can choose to sit in the front or behind me, I don't mind either way, providing you're quiet and don't upset the pooch."

He took the front passenger seat.

I want to be ready to jump.

"Oh, for goodness' sake."

She checked to see what the problem was, only to break into a fit of giggles as she watched the dog licking Anthony's cheeks as if its life depended on it. "Don't be so soft, she likes you. Either that, or she needs the salt from your skin."

Not waiting for a response, Lyn pressed the accelerator ensuring the Land Rover slipped to the left courtesy of the road camber, as they began their journey back to Stanton Hall.

"Will you be careful?"

"Will you be quiet," replied Lyn giving her friend one of her head-teacher looks.

Several minutes later they arrived at a road junction. Lyn was just about to turn right when something caught her eye, closing quickly from the left. A police car, its lights flashing and siren blazing, quickly passed across them.

"Watch out, Lyn."

"I saw it, it's okay. You know, I think that's Peter Riley's car. I wonder if he's on his way to Stanton Hall?"

———

"TURN AROUND, THERE'S A SHORTCUT WE CAN TAKE."

Lyn gave him a confused look." There aren't any other roads off this lane?"

Anthony pointed to a field gate several yards behind them. "We're going to cross-country. If he is going to the

Hall, we should get there before he arrives. It'll be a bumpy ride. Are you sure you want to drive?"

Lyn turned the vehicle after moving forward and reversing several times, and headed towards the gate. "I told you, you're not getting your hands on the steering wheel, so just tell me where to drive."

"Through the gate and straight on. There isn't any water between here and the Hall, so there shouldn't be any unpleasant surprises under the snow. You'll find the gap we can drive through in a corner of every field we need to cross, so keep your eyes peeled."

Silence fell as Lyn concentrated on throwing the Land Rover forward on its quest, the vehicle's four-wheel-drive facility coming into its own. Now that the snow had stopped and visibility improved, they were both able to take in the incredible vista of a patchwork of fields, each surrounded by snow-topped hawthorn hedges.

In the distance, church steeples pierced the otherwise flat landscape, waiting for their congregations to attend midnight Mass. Powdery snow whirled around the Land Rover as it speedily covered yard after yard on its meandering journey back to the Hall.

———

"THANK HEAVENS YOU'RE BACK, YOUR FATHER IS CALLING FOR you."

Anthony drained of colour as his Aunt May greeted them both at the front door of the magnificent building.

No, no, it can't be.

He looked to Lyn for comfort.

"It's okay, Ant, let's get up to him. We can deal with what we know; at the moment we're in the dark.

They bounded up the Jacobean staircase and raced along the landing. Opening the earl's bedroom door, Anthony was almost too alarmed to look inside. He felt Lyn clutching his arm.

Please, Father, not yet.

Much to his relief, his father sat smiling in bed.

Thank heavens.

"There you are, you two. You have been neglecting me."

Ant was still finding it difficult to smile, such was his agitation. "So the police got your medication to you?"

The earl wore a puzzled look. "Police? Medication?" What are you talking about, dear boy? Anyway, where's Thorndike?"

His son gave a sigh of relief. "It's a long story, Dad, which can wait for now. When you've finished your Earl Grey, I'll tell you all about it. In the meantime, I told you about Percy?"

The earl stopped drinking and placed his bone China teacup back into its saucer. "Still no sign?" His visitors shook their heads in unison. "I'm sure he will turn up soon, you know what he's like."

Before either could ask further questions, the bedroom door opened and in walked the butler. "I have brought you a little light refreshment, your lordship." The man expertly slid a silver platter of sandwiches and cakes onto the bedside cabinet.

"David, if you bring me any more food, you'll have my dear wife to answer to. I'm more than happy to scoff cook's wonderful cakes. However, Lady Stanton takes a dim view of my expanding waistline." He winked at the butler.

David held a white-gloved finger to the side of his nose. "Not a word, my lord." Seconds later he had vanished as quickly as he had appeared at the door.

"We are so lucky to have David, you know. He's so loyal."

Anthony nodded. "As were his father and grandfather before him, I'm led to believe."

The earl picked up a piece of cake and bit into it. "That is correct, my son. As I say, we are so lucky," he replied, spraying bits of cake over his eiderdown.

"Gerald, you are a one. Look at the mess you're making."

All three laughed as the earl tried to hide the evidence by brushing the crumbs off his bedspread with the side of his hand.

A few moments of silence fell as Ant's father enjoyed the rest of his snack before raising the subject of his uncle again. "What do you think Percy is researching?"

His father licked his lips to gather up the last of his cake. "He's been at it for years, Son. What he doesn't know about Stanton Hall and the two families that have occupied the estate since they built it, isn't worth knowing."

"So, no hidden treasure, Dad?"

The earl cocked his head to one side. "That rather depends on what you regard as treasure, darling Son."

What a curious answer.

"What do you mean?"

The earl picked up his tea and emptied the last of his drink, before returning his cup and saucer to his bedside table." It seems he's lately taken an inordinate interest in the Purple Lady. Heaven knows why, it's only an old wives' tale... I'm sorry Lyn; that was a dreadfully sexist remark, but you know what I mean."

Lyn gave the earl a fond look. "You're forgiven. It's interesting you mention her. As you know, we saw her this morning, and you explained when she normally appears. Perhaps there's more to the story than old wives, or anyone else is letting on,"

Anthony walked across the spacious bedroom to the window and peered out on the winter wonderland beyond. "Yet we still don't know what's happened to him, other than he's sustained quite an injury. Logic says he'd have headed for the hospital.

The earl ran a hand through his silver hair. "And that's the conundrum. If he isn't at the hospital, where is the man?"

At that moment, the phone rang. "Move the tray, will you, so I can pick that thing up."

Clearing the bedside table, she handed a cream handset to the earl. "Yes, yes, I see. Very well, I'll send them down. Thank you, David." He held the handset in midair. "It seems Detective Inspector Riley has arrived and wishes to see you both."

Rushing downstairs, David awaited their arrival in the hallway. "I have shown the Inspector into the morning room, sir."

Speeding towards the open door, they watched as Peter Riley paced around the exquisite room.

"Don't worry, Peter, we have your dog, just as we promised you."

Riley looked at Lyn as if she had taken leave of her senses. "Dog? What are you talking about? No, no, nothing to do with that."

"Then what is the matter, Peter?" asked Anthony.

Inspector Riley toyed with a pen between his fingers as if not knowing quite how to convey what he was about to say. "There's no use me beating about the bush. We received an anonymous call half an hour ago to say someone at Stanton Hall will be dead by midnight."

9

6:22 P.M. CHRISTMAS EVE

"I want a trace put on that call. Find out where it came from, do I make myself clear?" Detective Inspector Riley left no doubt he wanted results as he barked commands into his police radio.

Meanwhile, Ant and Lyn discussed what to do next.

"It could be a hoax call, Lyn. Probably someone tanked up and out to cause mischief."

"Yes, but the problem is, if it isn't, we're running out of time."

They exchanged concerned looks waiting for Peter Riley to finish his call.

"Not only are we running short on time; neither do we know who's at risk. Is it Percy? Your father? Or one of two hundred people who will be in these rooms tonight."

Ant looked around at the frantic pace of preparations for the Christmas Party as the house staff made sure everything was just as the earl and Lady Stanton required.

This is surreal.

Riley slipped his radio back into a jacket pocket and joined his concerned hosts. "That's all we can do for now.

My people think it's a local call, but until we can find a location, well... For the time being, I'll have a look around the Hall to see what jumps out at me."

Lyn couldn't help herself. "If you see a strange lady dressed from head to toe in purple, she's likely to do more than jump out at you."

Inspector Riley took several seconds to catch on to the joke.

"Take no notice of her, Peter. She spends too much time surrounded by seven-year-olds." He could see Lyn didn't appreciate his gentle put-down. "But you never know in a building as old as this, do you?"

I think I just about got away with that.

Riley shook his head in bemusement. "And what are you two going to do?"

"If Lyn agrees it's a good idea, I thought we might head back to the cottage."

"It'll be pitch black. What do you expect to achieve apart from us getting hypothermia?"

Anthony looked to the detective for support.

"I don't suppose it can do any harm, and the place isn't big enough for the three of us to be barging around in. That's agreed then, I'll look around here and you two catch frostbite."

I didn't realise he could be funny.

Within seconds Riley had disappeared, leaving the other two to deal with Aunt May as they made for a jib door.

"Doing your disappearing trick again by vanishing into the wall, I see, dear Nephew."

How much do I tell her?

Anthony smiled, trying hard to disguise his anxiety. "It's a perk of growing up in a place like this. From memory you have one or two secret doors at your place, don't you?"

I hope she bites.

"You are your father's son, as such I know so you're attempting to change the subject. You should know it won't wash with your dear old aunt."

Didn't think it would.

Lyn quietly pushed the jib door back into place just in case anyone came across them.

"If you must know, Lyn and I are heading over to Percy's cottage. We can't just sit here while he remains missing. We know he's injured, and the police—"

He felt Lyn's finger applying pressure to the middle of his back.

"You were saying, Nephew?"

Lyn took control. "He was about to say Inspector Riley is taking a discreet look around the Hall and see what turns up."

May gave each a sceptical look. "Is he? Meanwhile, you think you'll solve the puzzle of Percy's disappearance at that little cottage, do you? Perhaps I should come along?"

Oh no you don't.

"That's a wonderful offer, Aunt. It's just that, well, there's hardly room to swing a—"

"A wayward Uncle Percy around. Was that what you were going to say, my dear?"

Lyn couldn't help chuckling as the two women exchanged a mischievous smile.

"You have hit the nail, or should I say, Percy, on the head. Anyhow, you're much more valuable to my parents and me if you can keep the rest of the family occupied before the villagers arrive."

May wagged a finger at her nephew. "Young man. You are indeed your father's son. Be on your way. Go on, I'll close your secret door behind you."

Not waiting for a second invitation, Anthony stepped through the door, decorated to match the wall panelling of the corridor. Seconds later, Lyn followed.

"You mean to say in the old days, house servants spent their time scurrying up and down these horrible, dark service corridors?" Lyn waved her arms around to fend off a variety of imaginary and real insects.

Anthony hesitated in answering as he led the way towards a dim light at the end of the narrow passage, made possible because of a single small pane of glass in the door.

Anthony struggled to pull back bolts at the top and bottom of the old door, which had remained shut for decades. Once the door opened, a vicious stream of freezing air filled the dank space. "All I can say in defence of these Country Houses is that they created a great deal of employment. If our archives are anything to go by, estate staff enjoyed better health, at least the indoor staff."

Lyn huffed. "So that's all right then."

Anthony snapped back. "Don't be so childish, Lyn. That was then, this is now. It's no good pasting our morals onto a system that ceased to exist a hundred years ago."

Anthony didn't wait for her response. Instead, he stepped into the freezing early evening air, treading with care across pristine snow between the old buttery and laundry.

Lyn was in no mood to take his remarks on the chin. Following a few yards behind, she let fly. "Don't talk to me like that, Anthony Stanton. I know you're concerned for your father and Uncle Percy, but that's no excuse for being rude. Remember, it's me you're talking to."

Her companion stopped walking and turned to face her. Anthony hesitated before speaking.

I went too far.

"I'm sorry, Lyn. You're right. You know, there was a time when I could handle the stress. It seems that is not the case now." He walked towards Lyn until they stood within touching distance.

"The good thing is you're beginning to recognise things have changed since you came home from active service. You also need to accept it injured you. Not in the physical sense, but PTSD is serious, Ant. Now, give me a hug, you silly man."

The couple held each other close for the best part of a minute, their quiet interlude interrupted only by a lone fox barking in the distance.

"Come on, enough of this soppy stuff. Let's get to your uncle's cottage.

————

POWDERY SNOW PICKED UP BY FEET TRAMPING THROUGH THE winter whiteness caused a sparkling mist to proceed them as they neared the petite cottage. Finding themselves in the familiar surroundings of the small lounge, Lyn flicked a switch to power a single dim light bulb hanging from the low ceiling.

"What are we looking for?"

"That's the problem, Lyn, we won't know until we find it." A stream of condensed breath hung lazily in the chill air as each word exited its owner's mouth

Fifteen minutes passed as Anthony explored the upper floor, paying particular attention to the architectural plans that still lay strewn across Percy's bed.

Downstairs, Lyn checked each cupboard, drawer and shelf for anything that might give her a clue concerning what happened to Percy.

"Found anything?"

"Not a sausage, and all that congealed blood is giving off an unpleasant whiff. Is there anywhere else we can look?"

Ant thumped down the uncarpeted stairs and headed for the tiny kitchen. "Only the wash house and pigsty. Are you up for it?"

Lyn buttoned her coat and lifted its collar. "If I'm going to get frostbite, what better place than in a pigsty?"

Anthony laughed as he unlocked the insubstantial back door and headed into the dark. Lyn hesitated as she stood in the doorway, watching her companion approach the outbuildings.

"Come on, you. Or are you frit?"

Lyn pulled the rickety back door closed and followed in Ant's snow prints. "I'll show you who's frit, Anthony Stanton. Let's look in the wash house first."

Pushing open a timber slatted door that hadn't moved in years, Anthony gained access to the small space.

"You did bring a torch, didn't you?" asked Lyn.

I knew I'd forgotten something.

"Er, no need for a torch, my eyesight is excellent," he replied before tumbling over debris strewn across the floor.

"So I see." Lyn leant forward to help her best friend to his feet.

After several seconds, their eyesight became accustomed to the gloom of the bare-brick interior of the tiny building. In one corner stood a dolly tub, together with its wooden agitator. Next to it stood a stone sink supported by two substantial brick piers, and a single tap attached to the wall above the sink to provide cold running water.

"I wouldn't like to have spent my days in here."

Anthony watched a spider disappear down the plughole before popping its head back out to see what was going on.

"I don't blame you, but listen, there's nothing in here that can tell us anything about Uncle Percy."

Lyn stepped over the threshold and back into the crisp snow. "That just leaves the pigsty; come on or we'll be late for Father Christmas."

The prospect left Ant feeling cold. He hated pigs and feared their reputation for eating every scrap of anything they came across.

I know it's empty, but I'll still smell the beasts.

"There's nothing here either, Lyn. Come on, let's get back to the Hall and see whether Peter Riley has turned anything up."

Realising Lyn hadn't followed, he looked back to see what she was up to."

"Do you think ghosts leave bits of their dress for strangers to pick up?" Lyn held up a scrap of purple cloth."

Her companion sauntered back into the pigsty to see Lyn peering out of a brick-fronted shelter at the far end of the stile. "Where did you find that?"

"On a small hook that nearly took my eye out. Must have been cosy in here. That's if you discount the draft that is cutting my ankles off."

Anthony inspected the faded fabric. "As you say, ghosts don't leave bits of fabric all over the place. This mystery is beginning to feel like an episode of *Scooby-Doo*, and we know every episode ended the same way, don't we?"

Lyn picked the fabric from her companion's fingers. "They unmask the ghost that wasn't a ghost?"

"Precisely. The question is, does this fabric have anything to do with Uncle Percy's disappearance? And in turn, has that got anything to do with the telephone call the police took?"

Lyn teased several lines of stitching from the fabric. "Perhaps Percy was having an affair, the husband found out and made an anonymous threat to the police?"

Anthony laughed. "It's an intriguing thought, Lyn, and I'm not saying Percy's past it. But from everything I know of him, he's far more interested in dusty artefacts than the fairer sex."

Lyn shrugged. "I suppose you're right, but wouldn't it be delicious if it turned out to be a love triangle?"

He shook his head. "Love triangle, indeed."

———

"WHAT DO YOU THINK, AUNT MAY?"

Anthony waited for his relative to give her verdict on the small piece of purple material Lyn discovered.

"Well, it's old, and whoever made it knew what they were doing. It's of the finest quality. They've gone to the trouble of using a *detached stitch*. Look, you can see what I mean from what's left of this raised motif."

Lyn moved her companion to one side so she could inspect what May was pointing to. "It must have taken an age."

May nodded. This is something only the wealthy could afford to commission during the seventeenth century. There is a portrait in the dining hall that shows off the technique rather well."

Lyn brushed a finger over the delicate fabric. "Would that be the wife of the second earl?"

"That is correct; well spotted. My nephew here has taught you well."

Lyn glanced at Anthony and laughed. "I don't think art is his sort of thing. Old car engines, well, that's another thing altogether."

"Then it belongs to a ghost?" Anthony chose not to debate his disinterest in paintings.

May squinted at her nephew. "What a strange remark for you to make, my boy."

Before he could respond, Dr Thorndike appeared in the doorway to the morning room, while rubbing the sleep from his eyes. "My medicine, or rather, I mean your father's medicine. Has it arrived yet?"

Anthony looked at the butler who had followed Thorndike on his travels. "Have the police dropped the doctor's bag off yet?"

"They have, sir. Shall I fetch it?"

Thorndike turned around. "No, take me to it, I must give the earl his medication immediately. He's waited long enough. We must pray he remains healthy."

As Thorndike and the butler disappeared, Peter Riley rushed into the room. "We traced the call, do you two want to join me?"

———

"THE WHERRY INN?" ANTHONY FAILED TO HIDE HIS SURPRISE as Riley sped his two companions to the heart of Stanton Parva.

"It's a good job the snow has stopped, and the farmers are out clearing the roads, or you'd have had us in a hedge by now, Peter."

The detective half looked over his shoulder and smiled at Lyn." The police have influence, you know. These chaps must have known I'm in a hurry."

Anthony gave Peter a sly glance.

That's the second time today he's made a joke.

"I guess we are just lucky; the force has received a

weather warning to say another blizzard is on its way. We'd better not tell the farmers, or they'll take their tractors home and snuggle up for the night."

"The villagers will also like the break in the weather." Anthony pointed towards the partially steamed-up front window of the police car. "That's the first of them making their way up to the Hall. As good citizens, Peter, they're all on foot so they can have a drink."

The detective glanced at his front-seat passenger and smiled. "I'm glad to hear that."

General chitchat about the weather and what Peter was giving his dog for Christmas occupied the next ten minutes before they came to a stop outside the village pub.

High Street looked stunning as shop after shop, festooned with twinkling Christmas lights, illuminated the ancient village centre. At the bottom of a gentle slope, the village green enveloped its snow-covered Buttercross. A massive Christmas tree decorated with innumerable glittering baubles and flashing bulbs completed the festive scene.

Crossing the icy cobbled pavement with caution, all three ambled into the bar. The small space heaved with revellers engaged in lively chat and a variety of Christmas Carols. The cacophony caused the new arrivals to place their hands over their ears.

"Heavens above, what a din," shouted Peter.

"Every year it's the same, bless 'em," said Anthony.

"Wait till later tonight, you've seen nothing yet," added Lyn.

Recognising his new customers, the hostelry owner beckoned them to the bar.

It took a full two minutes for the trio to navigate through a throng of villagers intent on wishing them season's greetings. By the time they reached the bar, its owner had already lined up three glasses of whisky. "They're on the house. Happy Christmas."

Anthony quickly gathered his glass and took a swig. Lyn wasn't far behind, while Peter declined.

"I'm on duty, unfortunately."

"That's a shame, never mind," said Anthony as he split the contents of the detective's glass between Lyn and himself. "There will be some sore heads in the morning, Jed."

The pub owner laughed, though it was difficult to hear him above his raucous customers. "It's a sign of a good night out, isn't it? And it's good for my cash till. Also, it'll bring them back tomorrow lunchtime for my special hair-of-the-dog remedy."

Peter Riley leant on the bar so he could make himself heard without causing a kerfuffle. "I'm sorry to put a damper on things, but can you tell me if you still have a public telephone in here?"

Jed gave the police officer a confused look before doing the same to the other two. "Yes, we do. It's in the back."

"Has anyone asked to use it today?"

Jed's eyes widened. "Funny you should say that, Inspector. You don't get anyone asking to use it for twelve months, you know, not now everyone's got a mobile phone. Anyway, I've had two customers asking to use it today. I was thinking of having the thing taken out. It cost me a fortune to rent; now I'm not so sure."

Ant joined in the conversation. "You said customers, Jed?"

The pub owner gathered an empty pint glass from the bar and plunged it into soapy water. "Yes, they were customers, what else would they be?"

Lyn interrupted. "What this stupid man is trying to ask is if you knew either of them, or if they'd just stepped off the pavement, and disappeared again after paying you."

"Ah, now I understand; why didn't he say that?"

Three pairs of eyes concentrated their attention on Anthony Stanton. "What?"

Riley glanced around the packed bar before turning back to the proprietor. "I don't suppose either of them is still here?"

Jed plucked the pint glass he'd just washed and began drying it with a pristine white cloth. He raised his head to see over a sea of customers and nodded toward the far corner. "You're in luck, the last guy to use the phone is sat over there. He's been nursing a pint for the last hour and if it wasn't Christmas, I'd have chucked him out for costing me money."

Inspector Riley struggled to see the man.

"How lucky are you, Peter, that he's still here?"

"I think you mean how lucky are *we*, Anthony."

As all three began the arduous task of pushing their way through the merry throng, Anthony knew the man had noticed them.

He's going to bolt.

"We'd better be quick, he's off."

Outside, all three watched helplessly as the small, thickset man disappeared around a corner opposite the village green. Seconds later, someone cried out in pain.

Moving as quickly and as safely possible, the companions rounded the corner to see their quarry held in a headlock by Burt, Station Parva's desk sergeant.

Riley took a long look at the man who was struggling to release himself from the sergeant's vice-like grip.

"Get him to the station."

10

7:29 P.M. CHRISTMAS EVE

"Sit down and be quiet." Detective Inspector Riley spoke with force as he pointed to a stark wooden chair. "And I don't want you wasting my time, or you'll spend Christmas in a police cell."

"Should we be in here?" Whispered Lyn.

Anthony moved his head to the side so that he could speak directly into her ear. "Strictly speaking, no, not if Peter puts him under caution and informs the man that he's subject to a formal investigation."

The two friends sat quietly in matching chairs, set against a cream-and-brown-painted wall of the claustrophobic interrogation room. Peter Riley took his seat opposite the suspect. All that separated them was a small steel-framed table.

"What is your name?"

The man sniggered. "Jack Frost."

Riley tapped the end of his fountain pen on the Formica-covered tabletop. "I see, it's going to be like that. It seems you're keen to spend the next two days in one of my cells, with only the desk sergeant for company.

"You might like to know that he expects to be with his family this Christmas. If he must babysit you, I doubt it will please him, if you understand my meaning?"

The man shrugged. "So what, I don't know why I'm here."

Riley stood up and walked over to Ant and Lyn, giving each a solemn look. Turning back to the suspect, he sauntered the few paces necessary to stand immediately behind him and bent forward. "Last chance—name or cell. Your choice."

The detective's proximity and stern voice caused the man to jump. He soon regained his composure. "At least I get three hot meals a day here. What's not to like?"

Just then the interrogation room door opened, and a police constable stepped forward to hand Riley a small, folded piece of paper. Within seconds, the young officer had left the room, closing the door quietly behind him.

Riley discreetly flicked the note open and scanned its contents before refolding it. He shifted his focus back to the suspect. "It's so nice to meet you, Mr Bateman, or may I call you Jake, you know, seeing as we're friends now?"

Anthony watched from behind as the man shook his head.

"I don't know any Jake Bateman. Never heard of him."

Riley laughed. "Then you shouldn't have used your real name when you bought a raffle ticket in the Wherry Arms, should you?" The detective felt his pocket to retrieve a small clear plastic evidence bag. It contained the man's wallet. "Neither should you have left this when you made a run for it? A bit sloppy, don't you think?"

Bateman began to fidget. "I don't know what you're talking about."

Detective Riley slipped on a pair of forensic gloves,

opened the evidence bag and took out the battered black leather object.

Undoing a single popper, Riley opened the wallet and slipped out a credit card. "Well, well. What a coincidence. Do you know this card belongs to somebody called Mr Jake Bateman? What a small world it is."

Anthony turned his head towards his companion. "He's good, isn't he?"

Lyn agreed.

Riley asked the question again.

"Whatever," replied the suspect, his mocking tone causing Anthony to bristle with frustration.

"You made a call to this police station less than one hour ago. Why did you do that?"

"I made no call. I don't know who you've been talking to."

Riley pushed his chair back and placed his hands behind his head. "Funnily enough, the chap that owns the pub. You know, the bloke you asked if you could use his public phone."

Bateman laughed. "I think you've had too much to drink. I never asked that barman about a phone. Can I have something to eat, I'm starving."

Riley shouted for one of his officers instead of answering the suspect's request. Seconds later a young constable opened the door.

"I've had enough of this fool. Put the man in a cell pending further investigations."

As the constable took hold of Bateman's shoulder, forcing him to stand, Anthony had time to study his face.

No idea who he is.

Nearing the door, Bateman turned to Anthony. "Enjoy what's left of Christmas Eve, won't you?" He hesitated for a half second. "Then again, a lot can happen in a few hours, can't it, big man?"

"Get him out of my sight," barked Riley.

With the man gone, Riley closed the half-glazed door. "He's either an idiot that I can safely leave in a cell to cool off overnight, or we have a dangerous felon on our hands, and your family is at risk. My dilemma is which one is he?"

Anthony stood up to shake the detective by the hand. "That bloke leaves me feeling uneasy, but thank you for the way you handled that; quite impressive, I thought."

Lyn also got to her feet. "High praise indeed."

Riley blushed.

Looks like he doesn't often get compliments.

"We need to get back to the Hall, Peter. The villagers' Christmas party will be starting soon, and I don't want anything spoiling their enjoyment. Can you give us a lift back?"

Riley nodded as he reached the door handle. "I've a few things to tidy up here, so I'll get a patrol car to take you. I hope to be with you within the hour. Good luck."

The three companions exited the interrogation room and entered a short corridor leading to the police station's small reception area. Seconds later, the unmistakable sound of men arguing, and furniture being thrown around, echoed through the Victorian building.

"What in heaven's name..." Riley didn't bother finishing his sentence as he rushed forward.

Lyn and Ant followed.

I didn't expect this.

As they neared, several police constables were attempting to contain a scene of mayhem.

"What is going on?" demanded Riley.

At first, no one answered as the officers tried to regain control of four intoxicated teenagers.

"Do you need a hand, Peter?"

"A generous offer, Anthony. Grab any of these drunken buffoons you can." As he spoke, Riley launched himself into the melee.

Several minutes passed before order returned. Each of the miscreants now wore handcuffs, held firm by an officer, Detective Inspector Riley, or Anthony.

"Will one of you please explain why my police station resembles a zoo?"

Riley's question caused the drunken youths to begin murmuring to one another.

"Silence, I'll have no more of this nonsense in my Station. Not another word from you lot, do you understand?"

The space fell silent as the drunken men lowered their eyes to the floor.

"Constable Gibson, what is occurring?"

Ant looked at Riley in wonder.

What a wonderfully old-fashioned phrase, good on you, Peter.

Newly qualified Constable Gibson began his explanation, his voice belying his nervousness. "They were making a nuisance of themselves larking about around the Buttercross—beer bottles all over the place. I advised that they should go home to enjoy Christmas, and to give residents some peace. They declined to do so and began to sing a Carol, but using the wrong words, Inspector."

"What do you mean, the wrong words?"

The young constable released his grip on a handcuffed young man swaying gently from side to side. Taking out his police notebook, the officer read a page verbatim.

"Proceeding on foot down High Street at 18:55 hours, I became aware of certain noises emanating from the Buttercross. On closer inspection, I discerned four youths drinking beer from brown bottles.

"Upon advising them to disperse, they stood in a line and began to sing a Christmas Carol. I distinctly heard the following: 'While shepherds wash their socks by night.'

"I advised they were singing the wrong words and to go home. The one with blonde hair stuck his tongue out and blew a raspberry, which the other three then copied. Concerned for a breach of the Queen's Peace, I called for backup and accompanied them to the station."

The police officer closed his notebook and carefully placed it back into the breast pocket of his jacket.

A moment's silence fell as the four drunken teenagers continued to sway on their feet. Inspector Riley looked at his two guests before turning his attention back to Gibson. "Well, thank you for a most comprehensive report. You have made an excellent start to your career, which you can enhance by getting this lot in the cells. However, don't put them with the other one I've got locked up."

Less than a minute later, one of the constables rushed back from the cells and stood breathlessly in front of his superior.

"What on earth is the matter with you, man?"

The officer hesitated as colour visibly drained from his cheeks.

"Are you feeling ill, or is this a ruse to get time off over Christmas, because if—"

"No, sir, I er..."

"Spit it out, man, I haven't got all night."

"It's Bateman, he's—"

"He's what, Constable?"

Ant thought the young man was about to faint and moved forward, ready to grab him.

"Gone, Inspector. He's done a runner. I thought I'd locked his cell when all that palaver kicked off, so I came to help. He must have slipped out in all the confusion. I'm—"

"Don't bother saying you're sorry, Constable. I'm cancelling your Christmas leave so you may have time to reflect on your failings as a police officer. Now get out of my sight."

The young man needed no second invitation to withdraw from the Inspector's presence. He rapidly disappeared back to the cells as Riley turned to his guests.

Anthony spoke first. "That's all I need, Peter. Bateman could be anywhere by now."

Riley shuffled from one foot to the other. "I'm sorry this has happened. It's unforgivable, but at least let me arrange for a patrol car to take you home while I organise the search for Bateman."

Anthony hesitated. "Thanks for the offer, Peter, but it's okay, I'll sort the transport. See you later, ring if you find him?"

Inspector Riley nodded. " Of course. Be careful, both of you."

————

"ARE WE GOING FOR MY MINI, THEN?" ASKED LYN AS THEY stood in the chill evening air.

"No, I'll call a favour in from Jed. He has a Volvo four by four. It'll be safer on these roads than your car. Come on, let's get over to the pub."

The Wherry Arms took less than two minutes to reach on foot. Getting from the pub's front door to the bar took longer. "Come on, Lyn. Nothing for it but to push through."

Having to greet so many friends further delayed their passage. Eventually they arrived at the packed bar and found a few inches of space to catch Jed's attention.

"Who have you come to arrest this time. Don't you ever stop chasing bad 'uns?" Jed wiped his brow as he attempted to satisfy the demands of several half-cut customers impatient to be served.

"Jed, we need a quiet word with you. It'll only take a second." Anthony strained to make himself heard above the shouting and singing in the packed bar.

The pub owner shook his head. "You must be joking. Look at this lot, they'll riot if I disappear."

Lyn intervened. "It's serious, Jed. Two minutes, that's all."

Her pleading did the trick.

"Derek, get yourself behind this bar." Jed's roar shocked the pub into silence. "A favour, mate. Two minutes work for you. It's worth a pint."

Jed looked around the stunned crowd. "Happy Christmas, everyone. Keep drinking, I've a family to support."

Taking his lead, the crowd soon returned to enjoying both company and drink.

Pointing to the side of the bar, Jed led the way into a small sitting room at the back of the pub.

"Thanks, Jed, I owe you one," said Ant. "Two things—can you tell us anything more about the bloke we chased out of your pub, and may we borrow your Volvo?"

Jed laughed. "I assume your requests are in some way connected?"

Anthony looked at Lyn, his concern clear.

"What can you tell us?"

Jed rubbed his chin. "Well, he came in around six thirty.

He asked if I had a payphone and bought a pint. After that, I lost sight of him for a bit as the place filled up.

"Next thing I see is him coming out of the hallway where the phone is. He bought a couple of raffle tickets, then sat down where you found him. Anyway, you know him better than me?"

"Me?"

Jed shrugged his shoulders. "He's only been in the village a couple of weeks, but he works for you."

Ant looked stunned as he digested the news.

"I thought you knew everyone that works on the estate, Ant?"

Lyn's question stung.

I thought I did.

"Well, no time for that now, I can check the files when we get back to the Hall. Any chance of the Volvo, Jed, the roads are terrible."

The bar owner put a hand in his trouser pocket before handing over his car keys. "Don't damage it."

Ant laughed. "Damage the Volvo? If that thing was left in a layby, it would be towed away for scrap."

Jed extended his hand as if about to retrieve the keys.

"Okay, I get it. Yes, of course, we'll look after your car."

Lyn plucked the keys from Anthony's fingers. "We'd better go before he changes his mind. Thanks, Jed, you're a pal."

———

"THAT'S ALL WE NEED." ANT SIGHED AS THEY CAME TO A HALT outside Stanton Hall. A crowd of villagers awaited their arrival and were admiring the Christmas decorations and drinking warm mulled wine from porcelain mugs.

"They only want to wish the earl's son season's greetings. Come on, old misery guts."

Anthony threw Lyn a weary smile as he opened the Volvo's heavy door and waved at the villagers. "Happy Christmas, everyone. Great to see you all again. We're going to have a great night, yes?"

The villagers roared their approval before returning Ant's best wishes.

"Lyn, we can't hang around, I want to see how Dad is."

Lyn knew what to do. "Happy Christmas, everyone. We'd love to stay and chat, but I think you'd rather us make sure there is enough food and drink for you all. Am I right?"

A second roar erupted with several villagers holding their mulled wine up as a toast.

You're smart, Lyn.

———

"You're looking better." Ant's delight was evident as he and Lyn entered the earl's bedroom.

"And a good evening to you too. How did you expect to find me, pushing up the daisies?" Ant's father held his arms out in welcome as he sat in a comfy chair by the fire. "Give me a hug, both of you."

The earl's invitation didn't go unanswered as the pair took it in turns snuggling into Gerald.

"It was touch and go with your medicine. I thought we'd lost it for good, Dad. Still, all's well now, and that's all that matters. You look great."

The earl raised an eyebrow. "Not for long if your mother gets her hands on me. She's furious I hadn't some tablets spare like she always has for an emergency."

Lyn wagged a finger. "Lesson learned, I trust?"

Gerald nodded. "As you say." Anyway, now that you've checked I'm still breathing, you need to get downstairs and mingle with our guests. The last thing I want is the villagers suffering an overdose of the Stanton Clan. Your Mother and I will be down a little later. That means you two are Masters of Ceremony and all-round big cheeses."

———

"DOESN'T THE GREAT HALL LOOK FABULOUS?" LYN POINTED TO the swags of twinkling decorations and illuminated Christmas trees, which bathed the magnificent mediaeval room in a warm glow.

"I hate this bit."

Lyn gently eased Ant forward. "I thought Public School gave you the confidence to work a room."

"It did, but not the locals. All they'll want to know is the latest family gossip, and you know I always say too much. I'm worried I'll let something slip about Percy, never mind all the other stuff that's going on."

Lyn gave him a peck on the cheek. "Then you'll have to be a brave chap and bite your tongue, won't you?"

Before getting much farther into the room, a spontaneous round of applause broke out.

"Quaint tradition, don't you think?" whispered Lyn without making her words apparent to those nearest.

He lifted his arm and waved. "This is for my father, not me, which is how it should be. Come on, let's get on with it."

Lyn walked to the right, while Ant peeled to the left. In an instant, both were engaged in lighthearted conversations with villagers.

Anthony played his part to perfection in exchanging pleasantries. He knew the families of many in the room who had, for generations, enjoyed a close relationship with his family and the estate.

Noblesse Oblige. I guess we do have an obligation to the villagers.

"Did I notice Miss Blackthorn and you holding hands around the village the other day?"

The pointed question from Hilda Thwaite caught him off guard. "Well, er... from memory it had been quite icy, and I managed to steady Lyn a couple of times."

Hilda smiled as those nearby picked up on the conversation.

"And didn't I see you coming out of Lyn's cottage last Tuesday morning? It was rather early for a visit." Jasmin's pointed question stunned Ant.

And here's me thinking we were being discreet.

The timing of Lyn's arrival at Ant's side couldn't have been worse. "How is everyone? I hope you're all ready for the big day tomorrow."

A polite giggle spread amongst half-a-dozen villagers.

"Talking about the big day, have you two set a date yet? asked Hilda.

Ant blushed; Lyn coughed.

They were saved further embarrassment by the appearance of the butler. Whispering into Antony's ear, the earl's son fought hard not to show any indication of his alarm.

"Approach each family member, discreetly, David. Inform them all to meet me in the snooker room in fifteen minutes—without the children. And please, tell them they must not make their exit obvious," whispered Anthony Stanton.

11

8:11 P.M. CHRISTMAS EVE

A nthony looked surprised at how full the sizeable snooker room looked with members of the extended Stanton family, as they sat on long leather couches which lined each side of the room.

I didn't know there are so many of us.

Ant's parents and Lyn sat next to him at the far end of the room in an immense floor-to-ceiling hexagonal bay window. An illuminated Christmas tree in the grounds provided seasonal backlighting as snow fell, adding a fresh layer to the winter landscape.

Farther along the oak-panelled room, Aunt May occupied a seat nearest one of two open fires. Cedric sat opposite the formidable lady.

Those two will throw snooker balls at one another before the evening's out.

"Well, Son, you'd better tell them what all this is about before they turn on you and make for the eggnog."

Ant smiled at his father. "You may have a point."

"Serves them right, they're a selfish lot."

The earl turned to his wife and winked. "A perceptive

comment, my darling, but perhaps you might speak a little quieter. We don't want to offend the entire family in one go, do we?"

She narrowed her eyes. "You want me to answer that, my dear?"

Anthony joined in the quiet banter. "Behave, you two or I'll send you to bed without your supper."

The elderly couple chuckled to each other as his mother gave her son a playful tap on the back of his hand. "At least you had Nanny to slip you a cup of Ovaltine when I sent you to bed early. Yes, I knew all about that."

Lyn gave Ant a gentle prod. "And here's me thinking you were a little goody-goody when you were a child, when all the time you were in league with your Nanny."

Anthony sniffed the air in a display of nonchalant defiance.

The amusing interlude ended when a member of the family spoke up. "I assume there is a reason for penning us in here like sheep?"

Lady Stanton slowly got up from her elegantly upholstered chair. For such a frail lady, her presence still emanated a powerful force. "Be quiet, Cousin Wilfrid. To say this beautiful room equates to a sheep pen rather stretches the point. I suggest it's more fitting that we each thank our lucky stars we are so fortunate when others have little."

Lady Stanton's husband slowly rose from his chair and brushed her cheek with the softest of kisses. "You are magnificent, my dear. However, now you have shamed them into submission, perhaps it's time to allow our son to get on with things."

Anthony took the hint. "Thank you for leaving the party without creating a fuss. The reason for my rather strange request will become clear in a few minutes."

Twenty-one pairs of eyes settled on the earl's son.

"I assume all of you know that Percy is missing." He half turned to Lyn. "We've been busy trying to find him and dealing with one or two other matters, which are of no concern to you at the moment."

That didn't come out the way I intended.

"Shouldn't the family decide what is and what is not of concern to us, Anthony?"

I deserved that.

"I apologise. What I intended to say is that I think it better we prioritise our actions over the coming hours. You need to know the police have just told me they have received a credible threat that one of the family will come to harm before midnight."

The room erupted into a riot of sound as first one member of the family, then another, demanded more detail.

"Please, please let's all calm down." Anthony held his open palms out to reinforce his request. "We thought we had this matter under control because the police apprehended the man; they thought they had made the call. Unfortunately, he got away. I must be honest with you; we don't know his precise whereabouts."

Aunt May struck an imperious pose as she stood. "Do I take it this connects to the disappearance of my eccentric cousin?"

Murmurs rippled around the room.

"We just don't know. These are the facts. Percy arrived yesterday, he had dinner with my mother and father and later on undertook some research in the armoury.

"Lyn and I discovered him missing early this morning. An enormous amount of blood was present, and his car is missing."

A second member of the family spoke up. "You know

what Percy is like; he's probably in some dusty old barn counting tree rings or something to discover how old the thing is."

Anthony nodded. "Let us hope that is the case, although I have to say, given the time Percy has been missing, such an adventure seems less and less likely."

Cedric got to his feet. "Has the police tested the DNA of the blood you found?"

"That is a reasonable question, Uncle Cedric, and the police have it in hand. That it's Christmas Eve isn't helping matters, nor is the appalling weather. However, Detective Inspector Riley assures me he expects the results by the end of the day."

The room broke into disparate conversations on hearing the news.

"But what if the results don't come back in time? You said yourself, there is a madman out there threatening to kill one of us by midnight. It hardly engenders the Christmas spirit, does it?"

Anthony held out his hands again to quell the disquiet. "You're correct, Cousin. However, we are where we are, and that is precisely why I asked to see you all. All I ask is that we watch out for one another, if you see anything unusual to let me know and, above all, keep this from our guests."

———

ONCE FAMILY MEMBERS HAD LEFT THE ROOM, THE SNOOKER table again dominated the space. Gathered around one of the open fires, Anthony and Lyn reviewed the meeting with his parents. "What do you think, Dad?"

The earl peered at the burning embers, warming his outstretched palms courtesy of the fire's radiating heat. "Half of them were drunk so won't have understood a word said to them. Of those remaining, fifty per cent could not care less, leaving less than half a dozen who will do as you asked. Apart from that, I thought it went splendidly."

Lady Stanton gently tapped her husband's hand. "Stop teasing the boy, Gerald. I'm sure all will be well, and Percy will appear as if out of thin air."

Lyn snuggled into Ant to caress his arm. "Your mother says all will be well, so that must be the case."

The earl slowly got to his feet and assisted his wife to follow suit. "My darling wife is inevitably correct about such things, so I think we should join our guests and attempt to catch a modicum of the Christmas spirit."

Lyn offered the earl a cheeky smile. "Alcoholic?"

"You know me too well, young lady." The elderly gentleman returned Lyn's affectionate gesture.

Sauntering down the long room, Ant rolled a snooker ball over the pure green velvet of the table's playing surface. "Never had the patience for snooker. Billiards are much more my thing. More like American eight-ball pool, which I love."

"Darling Son, that tells me you spent far too much time in American bars for your own good."

Anthony giggled. "Just doing my bit for Anglo-American relations. When I was over there, I also got a taste for bourbon. Happy days."

As Lyn opened the wide panelled door to the snooker room, two surprised faces looked back at her. "Oh, I almost jumped out of my skin."

The butler acknowledged her with a single nod. "Apologies, madam. This gentleman arrived a few minutes ago asking to see Mr Percival Longbarrow. I thought it wise to seek Mr Anthony. Forgive my intrusion, my lord, Lady Stanton."

A tall, well-dressed man with a neatly trimmed moustache and rimmed glasses stood next to the butler. He extended a hand, which Anthony shook. "Welcome to Stanton Hall, Mr...?"

"Forgive me, my name is Dr Ian Philpott. Is Percival here?"

Ant looked at his parents and then at the new arrival. "Thank you, David, I'll take it from here. Please, Dr Philpott, please come in."

The butler took an elegant step back as Philpott entered the snooker room and sat on one of the long leather-covered benches.

"Forgive me, Dr Philpott; my wife and I need to say a few words to the villagers by way of welcoming them to our traditional Christmas festivities. I know my son and his dear lady will look after you well. Please, forgive us."

Dr Philpott immediately sprang to his feet out of respect. "Of course. Lord, Lady Stanton, a pleasure to meet you both."

Lyn once again opened the door and smiled as Ant's parents shuffled through on their way to the great hall.

"How do you know Percy, Dr Philpott?"

Philpott resumed his seat. "I'm a visiting professor at Cambridge University. Your uncle and I specialise in the same area and often collaborate." Philpott smiled. "Do you know, we always tease each other about the origins of our surnames. Mine originates from one of William the Conqueror's knights at the Battle of Hastings in 1066. Your uncle always teases me that his own goes much farther back. In fact, to burial rituals from the fifth-century BC. Do you know, the—"

"I'm sure that's fascinating, Dr Philpott. However, I'm confused. What brings you to Stanton Hall on a snowy Christmas Eve?"

Philpott looked up at Anthony. "Of course, I'm so sorry; I have a tendency to digress. Anyway, I received a call from Percy late last night. In fact, it was so late that I was fast asleep in bed. You can imagine my agitation at being disturbed.

"Imagine my surprise to hear your uncle's voice. The thing was, he sounded most agitated."

Lyn perched next to the professor. "Agitated?"

Philpott frowned. "Quite odd, actually. His tone was a mixture of excitement and anxiety, something I'd never heard from him before. Anyway, Percy mentioned he'd found something of significant historical importance at the Hall, but that someone was..." Philpott's voice trailed off.

Anthony shook his head. "Someone was what?"

"That is the issue, Lord Stanton. The line was awful. It cut out several times and eventually went dead. I assumed he'd ring back, but didn't. I tried returning his call but couldn't get through.

"It's most odd Percy was so imprecise. You know he is a highly regarded research fellow. It's not in his nature to beat about the bush or use vague language.

"In fact, I cannot recall a single instance when he has used the word, 'someone.' If ever any of his students use such loose terminology, he is the first to chastise them."

Anthony matched Lyn's look of concern. "You have no clue what he was talking about then?"

Philpott stood up and rested a hand on the mantel of the adjacent fireplace. "It's a mystery. I left things until lunchtime today, then decided I should come to the Hall to find out what is going on. From your tone and demeanour, I assume Percy is not available?"

Dr Philpott's host shook his head. "My uncle was last seen at dinner yesterday. It seems you may have been the last person he spoke to. He's raced off somewhere because his car—"

"Not possible, Lord Stanton."

Ant frowned. "I'm sorry?"

"Percy, his car. Your uncle would not have driven in this weather. It was fortunate it remained dry yesterday because had it rained, or, heaven forbid, snowed, he'd not have made the journey by car."

Lyn sauntered to Anthony's side. "Are you saying he never drove in poor weather, Doctor?"

Philpott shook his head. "That is the case, at least for the last twelve months. His eyesight is deteriorating. It's the price we academic researchers pay for spending decades poring over ancient manuscripts. Yet he blames the vagaries of the modern motorcar which, he maintains, are unreliable."

Anthony drained of colour. "That means he must still be somewhere in the grounds. Heaven help him."

―――――

"That is correct, David. Get as many men as you can to search every building on the estate. Make sure they have the correct clothing, radios, and torches. I don't want staff safety put at risk."

The butler calmly withdrew and closed the door to the snooker room as Anthony walked the few paces back to Lyn and Philpott. "This makes little sense. The Stanton Estate is large, but not so extensive one can disappear off the face of the earth. I don't understand what's happening."

Lyn tried to console her close friend as he looked out of the bay window onto a snow-covered landscape.

Dr Philpott joined his two hosts at the far end of the room. "Have you any idea what Percy was up to last night?"

Anthony spoke without turning to his guest. "He did what he always did when he came here, locked himself away in the armoury."

"Ah, I see. That makes sense because Percy mentioned the wealth of archives at the Hall many times. Please, would it be possible for you to allow me access so I may check what he was researching?"

A few minutes later, Lyn opened the heavy wooden door to the ancient room. "If anyone can make sense of this lot in Percy's absence, I guess it's you, Dr Philpott."

Philpott's eyes almost popped out of his head as he scanned the untidy room. Racing over to the pine table covered with parchments, he sat down, removed his horn-rimmed glasses and picked up one of the vellum documents.

"You found something?" Ant's tone was urgent.

Philpott slowly laid the parchment back on the cluttered tabletop and pointed to the cursive writing. "This is a letter from Henry the Eighth commanding the lady of the house to attend the funeral of his sister in fifteen thirty-six."

Anthony shrugged his shoulders. "And?"

Philpott tapped the parchment with a knuckle of his finger. "Fifteen thirty-six, Lord Stanton. That is the year in which his wife of over twenty-five years, Catherine of Aragon, died. Don't you see, he had divorced her to marry Anne Boleyn.

"It would have been impossible for the king to have

acknowledged Catherine as Queen. He then referred to her as his beloved sister. Here we have written evidence of that. Quite fascinating, don't you think?"

Lyn gently squeezed Anthony's hand. "Calm down," she whispered. "Something tells me he's the best chance we have of finding Percy alive."

Philpott remained oblivious to his hosts' quiet exchange. Instead, he concerned himself with a second parchment, its wax seal dangling from a silk ribbon central to the bottom edge of the ancient document.

"And this... This name—"

"I've had enough, Lyn. We haven't got time for this."

Anthony was already halfway out of the door as the academic spoke.

"No, you don't understand. I'm cert—"

"Let me know if you find anything relevant, Dr Philpott. Come on, Lyn, we need to get back to the party."

———

THE PARTY WAS IN FULL SWING.

"I reckon the band is competing with the villagers to see who can make the most noise." Lyn had to lean into Anthony to make herself heard."

He didn't answer; instead, his eyes darted from one part of the room the next, his attention shifting from one sudden noise to the next.

"Are you all right, Ant? You were a little short with Philpott, you know. Lyn linked arms to catch his attention. "Oh, look, there's Fitch."

Even mention of his good friend's name failed to shake Anthony out of his restless mood.

Lyn's persistence paid off in coaching Ant forward until they were a few feet from Fitch.

"You look happy. How much have you had to drink?"

"That's more than I can say for misery guts here, Lyn. He looks like he's lost a pound and found fifty pence."

Still, he failed to respond. Lyn gave Fitch a worried look. "I'm concerned about him," she whispered to the mechanic.

Fitch tried to engage his friend. "Now then, fella, I thought you liked Christmas. Look at all that chocolate cake."

Anthony turned his head from Fitch and concentrated on a narrow panelled door directly beneath the Hall's original mediaeval minstrel's gallery.

Just then several villagers barged into the trio as they excitedly made their way to the dance floor.

By the time Lyn composed herself, Anthony had disappeared. "Where's he gone?"

Lyn's plea caught Fitch's attention as he scanned the chaotic scene. "Beats me, but I bet he's vanished for some quiet. You know what he's like."

"You're right, I think I know where to find him. See you later. Oh, and yes, Maureen over there is giving you the eye. Don't leave it too long."

Fitch gave his friend a bemused look. "I've no idea what you're talking about."

Lyn laughed. "Is that right? Remember what I've just said. She won't wait all night."

Leaving the sound of the band playing a cover of Slade's "Merry Christmas Everyone" behind, Lyn moved quickly across the Hall towards the library. Stopping just short of the double doors to the impressive room, Lyn pressed the piece of oak panelling. This released a catch, allowing access to a tiny space that was once a projection room.

"I thought I'd find you in here." She moved inside and clicked the panelling shut. A single sixty-watt bulb illuminated the space, which measured three feet wide by ten feet deep.

Anthony toyed with an old cine projector, which pointed towards a filled-in recess in the library wall that gave film access into the library.

"Was it too manic for you in there? I know what it's doing to you, Ant. You need to talk."

"What is there to say? It is what it is."

Lyn landed a gentle kiss on his forehead. Making eye contact, she crouched down in front of him. "No, it doesn't have to be like this. You know PTSD is serious. We've spoken about getting you some treatment. It isn't a sign of weakness to ask for help."

Anthony filled up. "I was so looking forward to tonight."

Lyn leant forward to give him a hug. "It will be a wonderful Christmas party, I promise you. Will you promise me something?"

Anthony brushed his cheek against hers and buried his head in her shoulder. "What? His response was almost inaudible.

Lyn pulled away slightly so she could see his tear-stained face. "You make just one New Year's resolution. You promise yourself to get help because you can't go on like this. PTSD is serious stuff, and it will hurt you unless you protect yourself. Deal?"

What would I do without you, Lyn?

"Deal." The beginning of a smile spread across Ant's face.

She beamed. "I've got a great idea. Why don't we scuttle down to the kitchen and ask Mrs Smithson to make two mugs of her special hot chocolate?"

Anthony's smile broadened. "You know how to get to a man's heart, don't you?"

Lyn said nothing. Instead, she kissed his cheek for a second time, took hold of his hand and pulled him gently towards the secret door.

Within a minute they were in the white-tiled domain of Mrs Smithson. "Hello, you two. I was feeling abandoned down here now that the cooking's finished. Let me guess, hot chocolate?"

Lyn laughed out loud. "Honestly, are we that transparent?"

The cook returned Lyn's affectionate smile. "Neither of you have ever altered. Long may that continue. I didn't call you both chocolate tots when you were young for no reason, you know."

Mrs Smithson's recollection stirred a fond memory in Ant's subconscious.

I'd forgotten how innocent those days were.

All three settled around an immense table, bleached white with raised grain caused by decades of hand scrubbing. Seconds later the backdoor flew open, allowing a wall of blowing snow to precede two bedraggled estate workers.

"Get yourselves by the fire, you two," shouted Mrs Smithson. She walked over to an old Victorian range and made two more mugs of hot chocolate.

The men slowly took their white-caked gloves off, loosened their hoods and unwrapped heavy woollen scarves from around their necks. Holding their hands out to the warming flames, they seem lost to the world as they attempted to recoup body heat.

Ant noticed their pale pallor. "How long have you two been out there? You look ill."

The men slowly turned to the employer. Both hesitated to speak.

"What is it? What happened out there?"

Mrs Smithson gently placed a steaming mug of hot chocolate in their hands, which both men cradled as if their lives depended on it. Still, they looked at Anthony without speaking.

After exchanging another furtive glance, one spoke. "It was hard to make anything out in the trees, but it stopped to look at us."

Anthony frowned. "What did, a fox?"

Both men shook their heads. "There were no footprints in the snow, but she turned back to look at us, then moved down the side of the cottage and disappeared. It was as if she wanted us to follow her."

12

8:28 P.M. CHRISTMAS EVE

The unmistakable sounds of Christmas merriment made their presence known in the library as Detective Inspector Riley, and Anthony discussed the events of the day.

"How are you feeling now, Peter? That was a nasty bump on your head."

"My headache continues to remind me I'm not twelve anymore, and so don't bounce when I hit a hard surface. Other than that, I'm feeling fine."

His companion sauntered over to a hostess trolley on top of which rested a coffee percolator. "Then I'll save you the trouble of getting up. Coffee?" Before Anthony dispensed coffee, he grew curious about what warm delights might be inside the trolley. "We're in luck. Fancy a chicken leg?"

Riley smiled. "Yes, to both questions. They look after you here."

"Don't run away with the idea that the family gets this every day of the year. The staff reserve it strictly for the villagers' Christmas party. Still, it's a delightful treat."

Riley relieved his host of the hot drink and food before

settling back into his chair and tucking in. Anthony, meanwhile, crouched down to take a second look in the hostess trolley and squealed with delight. "Ah-ha, I didn't see the sausages. Leaving Peter to chomp on the chicken, he filled his plate with a variety of treats.

The two men exchanged light banter as they enjoyed the food before realities of the day's events came back to the fore.

"Can you recall many other days when one of your relatives has disappeared into thin air and your father collapses. On top of which you rescue the village doctor and a woman from a car crash, then have life and limb threatened by a madman?"

"When you put it like that," responded Ant. "No, I can't say it's an everyday occurrence. In fact, it's hard to recall such a strange day, even when on active service. The thing is, Peter, the whole thing seems surreal. At the heart of it, I have an uncle who may desperately need medical attention, yet we have no clue where he is."

"One thing is for sure, Anthony, he's not on the estate because we know his car's gone. I know you hear and see strange things in these old places, but motor vehicles don't vanish into thin air."

Anthony stood up and walked over to one of the large windows, which allowed daylight to flood into the reading chamber. Gazing over the formal gardens, letting his eyes wander into the snow-covered distance, he shrugged his shoulders.

"I hope you're right, Peter. If he's tucked up safely somewhere in the dry and warm, I don't care that he hasn't contacted us. Looking at this lot, the snow is getting heavier, which will be great for the children waking up to a white

Christmas tomorrow. Me? It fills me with dread. We have to find Percy."

Detective Inspector Riley sat forward and eventually released himself from his chair. "Is there anywhere nearby that he may have wanted to visit? As you said, his specialism is history, and there are plenty of places around here to keep him occupied. Perhaps he's gone to one of them?"

Anthony shook his head. "I don't think so. Percy gave his brother specific instructions. Even though the property was closed, it tells me my uncle knew exactly what he was doing. It makes little sense that he should just wander off."

"Anyway, I've got a speech to give, Peter, but please, grab me if any additional information comes your way. I'll be in the great hall."

———

EXCHANGING THE QUIET LIBRARY FOR THE HUBBUB IN THE great hall filled Anthony with anxiety.

This isn't like me.

As he ambled along the sumptuous Persian carpet that softened an otherwise austere panelled corridor, his heart raced.

If this is what a panic attack feels like, I'd rather be on active service.

With each step, the volume of noise increased. By the time he reached the majestic hallway of the property, Anthony felt faint.

I must get on top of this.

A sea of smiling faces and raucous laughter met him as he entered the great hall, which dripped with festive decorations and twinkling Christmas lights. Every sinew of him wanted to turn and run. The more he thought about panicking, the greater the panic became.

Anthony distracted himself by waving at the crowd and looking up to the great oak hammer-beamed ceiling. It was a tactic to stop the tingling sensation descending from his head, making its way down his arms to his fingertips.

I'm going to faint.

"There you are, Anthony Stanton, and here's me thinking you had abandoned us."

Thank you, Lyn.

He didn't speak. His eyes said it all.

"Hang on to me, Ant, I won't be moving from your side while you give your speech. You're safe, everyone here is your friend. Come on, hold my hand." Whispered Lyn so that no one around him could hear what she was saying.

Her words and touch did the trick. Anthony felt the panic subside as he digested her words and felt Lyn's comforting hand entwined in his. Finally reaching the far end of the immense space, they climbed the four steps leading to the stage together, at which point the crowd broke into spontaneous applause.

Lyn looked deep into Anthony's eyes. "Are you ready?" She whispered as he arrived centre stage.

"Yes, ready."

Anthony took the microphone from its stand and surveyed the crowd of smiling faces. "Ladies, gentlemen, children, and, oh yes, Fitch."

The Hall erupted into a roar of laughter as Fitch played along with being an afterthought.

"Each year for the last century and a half, the village has been kind enough to spend its Christmas Eve at Stanton Hall. Over the years there have been both high and low points. And by that, I mean locally and nationally, if we think about the tumultuous events that have played out over that one hundred and fifty years. Yet here we are again tonight. Still here, still laughing together and enjoying each other's company.

"And it's that which makes our community so unique. We rely on each other, we help each other, but I think more important than anything, we like each other. Changes are happening all around us and Stanton Parva isn't immune from that."

"Neither is my father's estate. However, one thing I can promise you is that my family will always be here to share good times and bad with your families."

"On behalf of my parents and me, may I offer everyone season's greetings. Happy Christmas to you all."

The crowd broke out into a second, more energetic round of applause.

As a villager arrived on stage, a stillness fell over the Hall.

Anthony and Lyn stepped to one side as the villager ascended the steps to the stage and joined them at the microphone.

"So, you got the short straw this year, Susan?" whispered Anthony.

"It serves me right for saying we're fed up with the men always doing it. Present company excepted, of course." The middle-aged woman dressed in a Santa Claus hat and trainers sprinkled with glitter smiled as she spoke. Accepting the microphone from Anthony, Susan turned to her audience. She hesitated for a few seconds, took a deep breath and lifted the microphone to her mouth. "Unlike last year when Frederick droned on for twenty minutes, I'm going to keep my response short."

The Hall erupted in laughter as heads swivelled to locate the unfortunate Frederick.

"Anthony told us how much his family appreciates us, and how far back the tradition of this get-together goes. Well, I'm here on your behalf to say thank you. In particular, to the earl and Lady Stanton, who have given so much to the village over the years. And to you, Anthony. We know how hard things have been for you over the last few years as you take up the reins from your parents."

"We want you to know that we are with you every step of the way. I can say that because we trust you. Trust you that in doing the best for the estate, you'll do your best for the village. So, without further ado, may I offer a toast to the Stanton family."

Instead of a glass, Susan held up a microphone. The audience returned the toast.

Anthony's eyes glistened as he listened to the toast. He felt Lyn's fingers pressing harder into his hand.

You always do the right thing, Lyn.

Susan was about to hand the microphone back when she hesitated and turned around to the audience. "Worrying about a member of the family is distressing any time of the year; at Christmastime it can be heartbreaking."

She turned back to Anthony. "All the village want you to know that we are rooting for your uncle to turn up safe. We think it's a measure of the earl and Lady Stanton's fortitude and courage, and your own, that you have allowed the event to go ahead. You may think we didn't know what was going on. Then again, villages are small places, and we care a great deal about you."

This time Susan's words met with polite applause, which grew louder and louder until the show of affection became too much for Anthony.

He turned away from the crowd and concentrated his gaze on Lyn. "Why are they so kind?"

Lyn gave him a hug, then a kiss. The crowd broke into a riot of whoops and clapping.

"When you admit you're loved, you'll be well on your way to recovery, Ant. I'll be with you every step of the way."

Together, they smiled and waved at the crowd, then walked over to the stage steps before disappearing into the crowd.

———

As they cleared the great hall and stepped back into the hallway, Lyn hesitated. "I think you need some time just for your parents and you. Find them and have a quiet ten minutes together. I'll be here when you're ready."

Not waiting for a response respond, Lyn crossed the black-and-white-tiled floor and disappeared around a corner.

She knows me better than I know myself.

Guessing his father had retreated to his bedroom, Anthony climbed the grand staircase. He made his way along the familiar landing corridor. Expecting to see both parents resting, his mother was absent.

Before he could reach his father's room, the butler, David, discreetly coughed to gain his employer's attention. "I thought you would like to know that the lady involved in the automobile accident this morning is regaining consciousness. I asked Dr Thorndike to call in on her."

"That sounds promising, David, and thank you for being so thoughtful and resourceful."

As he turned to leave, the butler coughed for a second time. "Is there something else, David?"

"Yes, sir, it concerns the gentleman who called upon us in a rather distressed state. Miss Blackthorn asked that I offer him a bath and fresh clothing."

"What makes me think a 'however' is about to crop up somewhere in your sentence?"

David cleared his throat. "As you say, sir. It seems the gentleman is missing from his bedroom, as are the contents of a decanter of whisky that I placed in the room only this morning."

Anthony rubbed his chin and smiled. "You're telling me we have a complete stranger who is as drunk as a lord on my father's whisky roaming about the place? Never mind, at least he will look presentable and smell a little fresher than some others I could mention this evening."

"Yes, sir," replied David, without making further comment.

———

"DO COME IN, SON."

Closing the door behind him, he turned to his father and smiled. "Both of you. It's hectic down there, and I thought it would be nice to spend some time with you."

"How are you coping, Son? You look unhappy, which is unlike you."

Ant thought for a moment. "I can't help thinking Percy's injured."

His father extended a hand to his son. "It may sound harsh, but what will be, will be. If the worst happens, it won't be the first time tragedy struck this house on Christmas Eve."

"You mean the Lady in Purple?"

"No, no, although the two events link insofar as both suffered persecution."

Anthony frowned. "Both?"

The earl leant forward to pick up a poker and jabbed at the coals, causing a rainbow of coloured flames to snake their way up the fireback. "Hundreds of years ago on a snowy Christmas Eve, not unlike this evening, a beggar turned up at the door asking for food and sanctuary."

"From your tone, I'm guessing this didn't end well."

"You're correct, my darling. The lord of the manor, who was a most unpleasant chap, forbade servants from feeding or giving the poor soul sucker of any kind and ordered the door slammed in the man's face.

"It seems several people recognised the man but were too afraid to question their master's instructions. The next morning, Christmas Day, the beggar was found frozen to death in a pigsty behind the head gardener's cottage. Poor soul must have crawled in there to get out of the weather."

Anthony, riveted by his father's tale, sat forward, keen to hear more. "Who discovered the poor chap?"

"The gardener heard his pigs making a commotion and went to investigate. Luckily for the dead man, though I doubt he could have cared less, he crawled into an empty pen. Had he gone into any other, the pigs would've eaten every bit of him.

"It turned out some servants were familiar with the man, and that he wasn't a beggar. In fact, he was a priest on the run from Elizabeth the First's men who were searching for him. By fifteen seventy, you may know it was dangerous to celebrate Mass. Had they found him, he'd have been executed, as would the lord of the manor."

"Do you think he recognised him?"

Anthony's father sat back in his chair. "After all this time, who's to say. What we know is that before January was out, the lord of the manor died, it's said from fright. Anyway, that's enough of the spooky stuff. Time to go find your mother before she gets lost. Then again, I've never seen your mother drunk no matter how much she drinks, which I've always envied. See you later, Son."

Left in the peace of his father's bedroom, Anthony's eyes felt heavy. Any danger of him dozing retreated as he heard a man's voice. There was was something vaguely familiar about it.

Where's that coming from, he sounds in pain?

13

9:07 P.M. CHRISTMAS EVE

I t must be the sash windows rattling in the wind.
Anthony discounted his earlier theory of hearing a man's voice and settled back into his father's favourite bedroom chair. As the seconds passed, so his eyes became heavier until the effort of remaining awake became too much.

I love my brother's car. I can't believe he let me borrow it. Greg is usually so precious about anyone getting their hands on his pride and joy. Bet it goes like the wind.

Why won't it move? I checked the petrol, and the tank was half full. I bet Greg is playing a trick on me. Perhaps he's not going to let me take it for a spin. That's just like my older brother.

What am I going to do? I'm already late for picking Uncle Percy up from the train station. He'll never believe that this big tree is stopping me from driving off. What if Percy thinks no one is there to collect him and gets back on the train?

Greg, don't be such a spoilsport, show me how to reverse your car so I can get it away from this ridiculous tree trunk. Greg? Where are you? You really are a pain when you want to be.

I hate being the younger brother. He always gets the girls.

Look at this purple coat. If they've gone for a walk in the blizzard, she'll be freezing, and I bet he won't give her his jacket.

Wait a minute, it's too warm for snow. I know this place; I've been here before with Greg, but it was raining hard, and he was asleep. Why did he tell me to come just so he could sleep?

Hello, Dr Thorndike; what are you doing here? Are you looking for my father? He's... Actually, I don't know where he is. I'm sure he said he was going to a party, but he didn't say where.

It's getting crowded here. Why is Lyn pointing her silly film projector at me? What does she want me to do, do a song-and-dance routine? Oh, thank heavens she's turned it off. I hate bright lights, and she knows that.

Too much noise. Where's all the shouting coming from? It's hot, all this sand? It will ruin Greg's engine. He'll never let me drive his car again. Why won't it move?

Where's the sun gone? I need to put the soft top up; it's starting to rain. I can't get out of the car. I'm trapped. That tree; it's getting closer, it's going to hit me. No.

Why does my head hurt? Blue lights, noise. Stop, please stop.

That's better. Just me and Greg.

I'm glad you're driving in this weather, brother. The rain is so heavy. Why aren't we moving?

I don't understand what you mean. That name sounds familiar. Is it one of our relatives? What do you mean? Greg, Greg, why are you asleep? It's dangerous when you're driving. Open your eyes, Greg. Wake up.

"Wake up. Wake up, sleepy bones," said Lyn, her calming voice trying not to alarm her best friend.

Anthony felt pressure on his shoulder and the sound of a familiar voice.

"Greg, come back. Don't go."

"Greg's gone, Ant. Remember, he crashed his car into a

tree. It's okay, just take your time, you're safe. I'm here for you."

"No, Greg is here. He's smiling at me." Anthony gradually opened his eyes and acknowledged Lyn's calming presence.

He gazed around his father's bedroom as if trying to orientate himself and distinguish reality from dreams. "We were together in his car just after he'd crashed. Greg wasn't in pain. He said he was happy."

Lyn crouched beside Anthony. "You had a stressful day, Ant, and you've had to cope with the flare-up of your PTSD. Perhaps your mind wandered as you slept?"

You weren't there.

"I know what you're thinking, Lyn, but I saw Greg as clearly as I see you. I told you how happy he said he was. Then he said something I don't understand. He said when we found Nicholas' work, we'd be happy too."

Lyn looked confused. "Do you mean St. Nicholas, as in Father Christmas?"

"I don't know, he said nothing about Christmas."

————

HAVING SPENT TEN MINUTES UNSUCCESSFULLY ATTEMPTING TO locate his mother, Anthony suggested to Lyn they should try the yellow sitting room. "You know it's her favourite hideaway."

Opening a wide panelled door with gold-leaf adorments, Lyn stepped into the intimate space. "I love the pastel shades in the Regency rooms. You'd think primary colours might be hard on the eye, but it works."

Her companion glanced around the room he'd been in a thousand times. "Well, wherever my mother is, she's not here. What say we hang around for ten minutes before going back to the party?"

Their solitude did not last long.

"Insufferable. The man is insufferable." May's cheeks flushed crimson with rage as she barged into the sitting room and flounced into one of the silk-covered sofas, still muttering under her breath.

Lyn sauntered over to the door and closed it to afford the irate woman a modicum of privacy. "Shall we leave you alone, May?"

Smoothing the creases from her dress in a fashion more suited to beating a carpet, she shook her head. "I had intended to escape this madhouse for a spell of solitude. However, I'm reminded that you two, apart from myself, of course, are sane. Therefore, I welcome your company."

"Might I venture to guess that the focus of your irritation is Uncle Cedric?" said Lyn.

May's cheeks flushed again at the mention of the man's name. "That man is a hypocrite. Yes, that's the right term: a hypocrite."

Lyn wandered back across the room until she stood next to Anthony. "What has he done to annoy you this time?"

"I came across him slouched in a corner, looking downcast. At first, I had no intention of engaging with that so-called gentleman. However, as is my way, my generosity of spirit got the better of me."

Anthony tried not to giggle.

And modest with it, Aunt.

"Well, Aunt May, his brother is still missing, and I'm sure we are all worried sick about him, even you?"

Ah, from the look you're giving me, I guess not.

"Your uncle had the gall to say if only he had kept in

touch with his brother, then perhaps the events of today mightn't've taken place."

Lyn stepped across the oak herringbone floor to take a seat next to May. "Who knows, perhaps that's true."

"Twaddle. Percy is the most selfish man ever to have walked the earth. He cares for nothing except his silly research."

This is getting out of hand.

"Aunt May, I can see that you're angry, but please, Percy may be in harm's way. Why are you so angry about his research?"

"Because if he hadn't had done so much digging, I would have married the man I loved." May rung her hands together before retrieving a handkerchief and dabbing her cheeks."

Anthony reeled at the sudden outburst and May's show of emotion.

I've never seen her cry before.

He wasn't quite sure what to do.

Lyn attempted to put an arm around the distressed woman. "I'll have none of that soft-soap nonsense, I..."

Raw emotion overcame May as she collapsed into Lyn's waiting arms.

Whisky, that's the thing to do.

Pouring a healthy measure of the single malt into a beautifully cut lead crystal glass, Anthony knelt in front of his relative and held out the drink. "This will help, Aunt May."

Dabbing a cheek for the second time, May glanced at the whisky before shaking her head.

I'll have it then.

He downed the twenty-five-year-old vintage in one gulp. Catching his breath at the sudden intake of strong alcohol.

"Do you want to talk, or shall we just sit quietly?" Lyn spoke with the gentleness meant to soften the hardest of hearts.

May relaxed her grip on Lyn and sat back into the sumptuously upholstered sofa. "His father was a gambler—the horses. I ask you, what sheer hypocrisy for this family to take against such a man. Our own wealth and influence derived from the turn of a single playing card."

"What has that got to do with Uncle Percy?"

May began to tear up again, but quickly got control of her emotions. "The family had suspicions about my Roger's father. He was a common sight at every racetrack in the land. Naturally, they thought his son was a gold-digger.

"You know how it goes: the father who has gambled away the family fortune orders the son and heir to marry into money. Roger knew what havoc his father was causing. Our plan was to get married and immediately elope with his trust fund intact. Yes, Anthony, Roger was, and remains wealthy, but knew he had to clear off before his father frittered his trust fund away."

Well, well, would you believe it?

"I assume Percy was doing what he was told to do?" asked Lyn.

May shook her head. "That's not the point. We were friends, we grew up together. Why couldn't he have shared the family's concerns with me instead of ruining everything? I'd have told him, but no, the thrusting junior researcher assumed he knew better, except he didn't."

Lyn turned to a small coffee table next to the sofa on which stood a sealed bottle of still water and two upturned glass tumblers. This time May accepted her host's hospitality.

"Why didn't you protest, Aunt May?"

"Because it would've been futile. Women may have got the vote in 1928, but even decades on, it was still a man's world, as it remains today in so many ways. Anyway, they made sure they put a stop to the wedding."

Lyn poured a tumbler of water, took a sip and placed her glass back onto the coffee table. "Did you try to keep in touch with your fiancé?"

May once again shook her head. "He was as heartbroken as me, so left the country soon after. Years later I read an announcement in *The Times* he'd married, so that was that. I occasionally pick up snippets about his life. Roger remains happily married with four successful grown-up children. So at least one of us found happiness."

Anthony poured another whisky, which again he downed in one go. "You must hate us all, Aunt May?"

Several seconds passed. "Yes, except for your parents, who were the only people ever to show me kindness and understanding. And, of course, the new generation who know nothing of what happened. Other than that, yes, I despise them."

Ant and Lyn exchanged an urgent glance.

"I know what you two are thinking, but it's an enormous step from loathing someone, to killing them. But then, I'm not the only one that Percy has hurt, or can ruin."

"What do you mean?" asked Lyn.

"The wretch has put his long experience and research expertise to good use. I suspect he learned a great deal from his shortcomings over my wedding, but if I know him, and I do, he knows where all the family skeletons are buried. Maybe he pushed it too far with one of them, and they resorted to a spot of instant justice?"

"AND WHERE ARE YOU WANDERING OFF TO?" LYN HARDLY recognised the man walking towards her as the unkempt beggar of a few hours earlier.

Dressed in blue corduroy trousers, a matching shirt and pullover, the stranger's rejuvenated appearance was complemented with a smart pair of black shoes and Father Christmas red socks.

"I've been trying to find my way out for ages. Anyway, all these things look the same." The man flicked his finger to denote the long corridor lined with oak panelling and a variety of Stanton family portraits.

Lyn took a step back, having caught a powerful aroma of whisky when he spoke.

I think you've had one too many over the yardarm.

"You're right, there; I've been coming here since I was a young girl and still get lost. I bet this place could tell a few tales. Don't you wish these walls could talk?"

The stranger gave a long blink before turning to face a wall, before turning back to look at Lyn, almost losing his balance as he did so. "They say nothing to me. What about you?"

Lyn smiled. "I didn't mean literally... Anyway, never mind about that. What are we going to do about you?"

Stretching out a hand to steady himself, he slumped onto one of several ebonised chairs that lined the corridor. "About me? What you mean?"

Grabbing hold of another of the chairs, she sat next to him. "Do you make a habit of knocking on strange doors in the middle of a blizzard?"

The stranger lolled from side to side as the whisky did its work. "Is it snowing? I didn't notice. One minute I'm nice and cosy in my... Wherever it was. The next minute a strange man and woman are pulling me into the house." He tried to turn his head to take in his surroundings but thought better of it as his centre of gravity shifted to one side.

"That woman was me. As for the man, he's the butler to this noble house."

Is he playing a joke at my expense, I wonder?

"And that wasn't the worst of it. That man stood over me while I took my best clothes off and told me to get into the bath. You know that water can be bad for you, don't you?"

Lyn couldn't help laughing. "Your best clothes?"

The stranger tried but failed to maintain eye contact as he nodded. "As for water, anyone would think you came from the Middle Ages. They avoided water as much as they could."

He raised his head to meet Lyn's gaze. "Last time I was here, it wasn't a problem."

The man's reply confused her.

What's he playing at?

"So you've been here before?"

The stranger fumbled in his trouser pocket. After a few seconds, he pulled out the small silver crucifix Lyn had watched him conceal in the hallway when they first met.

"See, I got this." The man tried to focus on the small silver artefact in his shaking hand."

"You picked that up a couple of hours ago, I saw you."

The stranger shook his head. "No, no, they gave me this last time I visited. Anyway, if you let me keep this, I'll give you these." Reaching into a second trouser pocket, he retrieved a row of twelve wooden prayer beads, strung onto a delicate string of leather.

"They're so simple but exquisite and must be precious to you?"

"I suppose it's only fair if I'm allowed to keep what they

gave to me, you ought to receive something I left here a long time ago."

What is he talking about?

"Sorry, I don't understand."

Suddenly the stranger's demeanour changed. All signs of drunkenness disappeared, to be replaced by the gentlest and most serene look Lyn had ever witnessed.

Why do I feel so peaceful?

Gently extending a hand to cradle Lyn's upturned palm, the stranger draped the silver crucifix over her fingers.

That smile again. Who is he?

"Don't forget to follow the lady, Lyn."

As he spoke, she felt compelled to close her eyes.

Why don't I need to ask him why?

When Lyn opened her eyes, she was alone. In her right hand, the crucifix swung gently on its delicate chain.

I don't know why, but I must get to the armoury.

14

9:39 P.M. CHRISTMAS EVE

"I agree, my darling, the debacle over May's wedding continues to cast its ugly shadow over this family." Lady Stanton nursed a cup of her favourite chamomile tea as she listened to her son explain his shock at his aunt's sudden outburst.

Straddling a simple beech chair in the tiny second-floor kitchen used by the family when there was no staff at the Hall, Anthony hung on his mother's every word. "And Dad and you never talk about what happened?"

"There is no sense in digging up old bones. In any event, I had my own problems when I joined the family. It wasn't easy; something your father is well aware of."

"I didn't know that. What happened?"

His mother sighed. "I didn't come from "old money." Your grandfather made his way in the world and did very well. I benefited from that. Unfortunately, families like the Stantons don't attach the same value to money earned from what they call "trade" as from landed estates."

Anthony failed to hide his shock. "Mum, I'm over thirty

years of age, and it hadn't occurred to me that such prejudices still existed?"

His mother chuckled. "Thankfully, your father and I
don't subscribe to such nonsense. That's the way we brought
your brother and you up. You not seeing such prejudice is, I
suppose, a testament to our success."

Her son played with the lid of a half-full bottle of tomato
ketchup that sat on the small melamine-covered kitchen
table. "Yet they pretend everything is always hunky-dory."

The mother wagged a finger at her son. "I remember
telling you off for doing that when you were young."

"What?"

"Scraping the tomato ketchup from the lid. You were
always such a messy eater. Naughty boy!"

*Why do we always revert to being a child when in the
company of our parents?*

"Anyway, about putting on a front. Well, that's what
families like ours do. Always pretend everything is as it
should be and never show weakness. I suppose that's where
the term 'a stiff upper lip' came from."

"And the misery that comes with it?"

Lady Stanton held out her cup. "Make me another tea
will you, my darling. All this talk of the Stantons fills me
with the need for more soothing chamomile."

Anthony replenished his mother's cup and took a seat
back at the circular kitchen table. "You didn't answer, Mother."

The elderly lady blew over the hot drink before
engaging her son with a severe look. "They can't help themselves. Their parents and grandparents experienced times of
great privilege and loss in equal measure. All this in a world
that changed out of all recognition in their lifetime. It
doesn't surprise me at all that many are bitter."

Enduring active service and losing close colleagues is just as hard now.

"But are people like May and Cedric bitter enough to kill?"

Lady Stanton's eyes bore into her son. "Everyone of us, without exception, can do the most horrendous things if provoked. What form that provocation takes will vary from person to person.

"Those who say they couldn't do 'such and such' delude themselves. You, above all people, know this to be true. Remember what you have seen and, no doubt done, in the service of Queen and country."

This is making me feel uneasy.

Anthony stood and took the few steps necessary to reach a kitchen cupboard to retrieve a round biscuit tin decorated with scenes of London Bridge and the Houses of Parliament.

Prising the stubborn lid off the container, he retrieved two chocolate digestive biscuits. "Your assessment concerns me, Mother. If you're correct, it means Cedric and May, working alone or together, may have done something terrible to Percy. Frankly, I don't know what to do next."

"One thing you can do is to cease addressing me as 'mother,' a term you have addressed me by twice in as many minutes. It usually means I have incurred your displeasure, you have done something wrong or are feeling anxious. I believe it to be the latter. However, my dear son, stop it."

Now I understand why adults feel like children in front of their parents.

"Sorry, Mum." Anthony sounded like a child being grounded by a disappointed parent.

The matriarch of the family grinned at her wayward son. "Quite right too. But to be serious, let me say this: when you were on an intelligence mission and things went wrong, what did you do?"

What does she mean?

"Come on, quickly; you're a soldier, what did you do?"

He thought for a few seconds before he realised what his mother was driving at. "I would test my original planning assumptions against the changed circumstances, then act accordingly."

Lady Stanton beamed at her son. "Then, my darling, you know precisely what to do next."

———

"SO THAT'S WHERE YOU HAVE BEEN HIDING." ANTHONY playfully pointed a finger at Fitch, who had his arm around the lady he'd been too shy to approach earlier.

"You can talk; you've been like *The Scarlet Pimpernel* for most of the day. One minute you're here, the next you've vanished. Anyway, when I caught sight of a bloke coming down the stairs, I assumed it couldn't be you because Lyn wasn't with you."

Fitch turned to his female acquaintance and gave her a peck on the cheek. She responded in a similar vein.

"We're not joined at the hip, you know. I have a life of my own, as does she."

"You could have fooled me. You two are at the point now that you finish each other's sentences. It won't surprise me if you've got a pair of slippers and a pipe hidden somewhere at her place."

The object of Fitch's observations became eager to change the subject. "And am I to be introduced to your companion?"

Good, that put you on the back foot.

Fitch smiled at his companion, then turned to Anthony. "Lord Stanton, may I introduce you to, Sophie, a spinster of this parish and an all-round good egg."

The woman pinched one of Fitch's earlobes between finger and thumb. "Less of the spinster, my little oily rag." Her fingernails had the desired effect in making Fitch wince."

"My little oily rag? That's a new one on me. I see you in a completely different light." Ant crossed his arms and smirked like a head teacher getting the better of a cheeky teenager. "Anyway, may I have a word with you?"

Fitch's smile disappeared. "What, now?"

"Please forgive me, Sophie, I wouldn't be dragging this, er, oily rag from your company if it wasn't urgent."

Releasing his affectionate embrace, Fitch attempted to plant another kiss on Sophie's cheek.

"Oh no you don't. I don't mind you being dragged away by the lord of the manor, just don't expect me to be here when you come back. It's Christmas Eve."

Oops, didn't mean to do that.

Fitch hesitated before realising Sophie had a twinkle in her eye. "I promise I'll be five minutes with this fool, lord or no lord. You wait there, and I'll get someone to bring a refill, okay?"

Sophie's broadening smile lanced Anthony's guilty feeling as he led his friend to the corner of a temporary bar, set-up especially for the party.

This time the loud cacophony of music and revellers deep into the festive spirit had no effect on Anthony's mood. He listened to his mother's advice and knew what he had to do.

"Are you sure Sophie is keen on you? Oily rag doesn't sound like a term of affection to me." Anthony took possession of two bottles of Fen Bodger pale ale, handing one to Fitch.

"We have nicknames for each other. I'm a mechanic, so, oily rag, get it? Sophie is a midwife, so I call her—"

"In that case, I have no wish to know. Just drink your pale ale and think about what Father Christmas is going to bring you."

Fitch took a swig of his drink and made as if he were choking. "You did it on purpose, you know I drink lager, not this mucky stuff." Wiping the remains of the pale ale from his lips, Fitch looked at the bottle with disdain before sliding it onto the wet bar top. This caused the glass container to fall and crash to the floor with an explosion of agitated alcohol.

"Well done, Fitch; my staff will think you're wonderful for making more work for them."

"Oops, didn't mean to do that, but it's your fault for feeding me that stuff. Perhaps you did it on purpose?"

"Me? Never," replied Anthony, his smirk giving the game away.

Replacing Fitch's discarded drink with a can of lager, his companion's voice took on a more sombre tone. "I wanted to have a word with you about that Jake Bateman bloke. Do you know anything about him?"

Fitch lifted the aluminium tab on his lager and pushed the open flap into the can before taking a long swig. "I only spoke to him once, and briefly at that. He came into the garage to ask if I had a five-litre can of engine oil.

"I had my head in an open engine compartment mind, so when I suggested he hang on for a minute until I finished what I was doing, I didn't expect the reaction I got."

"What you mean?"

"He flipped from a normal bloke to a crazyhead in a split

second. I thought he was going hit me." Fitch shook his head and downed another swig of his lager.

"You're joking?"

"That's the problem, I thought he was until I caught sight of his bulging eyes and clenched fists. He got as good as he gave, mind. I told him if he didn't behave I'd chuck him out, head first."

"Was it then that he thumped you?"

Fitch shook his head. "That's the strange thing. He backed off and calmed down as if nothing had happened soon as I challenged him. A right creepy guy who I wouldn't want to meet in a dark underpass if you know what I mean?"

How did we come to employ him in the first place?

Although the great hall bulged with happy revellers, Anthony felt strangely alone.

"Are you okay, mate?"

"Sorry, Fitch, I'm miles away. How come I didn't know he worked for us?"

Fitch placed his almost empty can of lager on the bar top, this time making sure it stayed where he put it, before resting a hand on his friend's shoulder. "You can't know everything that goes on. From what I understand, he worked on one of your father's forestry workshops miles away. You give your managers the flexibility to hire and fire?"

"Yes, provided they stay within budget and deliver the return on investment we expect, they run their own operation."

"There you have it. A local manager replaces or decides he needs an extra pair of hands and gets on with it. How could you have known? You do have a habit of beating yourself up, Lord Stanton. You can't be responsible for everything and everyone on this estate.

That's easier said than done.

Anthony swirled the last of his pale ale, causing it to froth in its bottle before emptying it in one gulp. "The thing is, Fitch, do I treat his telephone call to the cops and subsequent escape from the police station as a lucky drunken fool and harmless, or treat him as a threat?"

Fitch shrugged his shoulders. "Do you think he knows your Uncle Percy? Could he have a grudge against him? Either way, I'm not sure you can afford to take the risk. At least not until your relative turns up safe and sound."

"I agree, the problem is how to protect the best part of two hundred people against a nutter working alone?" Anthony scanned the festive scene around him and shuddered.

"You need not worry about this lot, Ant. If he's coming, he's after your father or you."

Everything points to Jake Bateman. But whatever he's done, the man is confident his prediction will come true. Why else would he sit in the pub knowing his telephone call would be traced?

Why risk being arrested? Bateman couldn't have known he'd get the opportunity to scarper from his cell. Why does none of this make sense?

Anthony walked towards the old head gardener's cottage. Although the wind had moderated, the snow was still heavy, yet he didn't feel the cold as his mind raced.

Percy drives all the way here, yet Dr Philpott says he won't travel in poor weather. A man makes a hoax call suggesting death and is on the loose, yet there is no credible evidence he means harm.

And why does everything come back to the cottage? Blood on the floor, but we don't know yet who it belongs to. A bed not slept in and instead covered in blueprints as old as the Ark?

Anthony showed no reaction to the seasonal scene of white-frosted Christmas trees, their lights twinkling as snowflakes floated gently past. His eyes focused on the silhouette of an isolated cottage.

Tell me what you know. You saw whatever happened here after Percy arrived. If he has come to any harm and I could have done something, I'm not sure I could live with that.

Flinging the garden gate open with rage-driven force, the construction this time gave little resistance. As it moved back, it pushed a deep layer of snow before it. Caring little whether he'd slip on the sloping path or not, Anthony clattered through the front door and stood alone in the cold, dark, living room of the tiny dwelling.

What were you looking into, Percy? What on earth was so important that it was worth all this worry and concern for you?

Watching his breath instantly condense to form a cloud of moisture before disappearing into the snowy night air, Anthony moved through to the kitchen. He opened every cupboard, every drawer and every container.

Nothing, zippo. This is a waste of time.

Dejected, Anthony slouched back into the lounge to take a last look around. He opened a small, sharply angled door that enclosed a cupboard under the stairway. Kneeling on all fours to clamber inside proved futile as it became clear the small space was empty.

Still on his hands and knees, his head crashed against the tiny door frame.

For the love of... Ouch, that hurt.

Hitting his head caused Anthony to stumble backward as he instinctively ducked under the low door frame while rubbing the back of his head.

Realising all he could do was extend his arms behind him to steady himself, he cried out in pain as his right palm landed on a sharp object.

Ow, what in heaven's name is that?

Finally getting to his feet, he was unsure which hurt more, his head or hand.

Glass. I hate that stuff.

Checking the cut to his palm, Anthony couldn't believe what he was looking at.

A diamond? What on earth is a diamond doing here? Is that what this is all about?

15

10:18 P.M. CHRISTMAS EVE

Anthony ambled out of the old cottage without bothering to close the front door, so engrossed was he with the exquisite diamond resting snugly in the palm of his hand.

Am I making two plus two add up to five, or did someone hide it away years ago? Then again, how did such a precious object come to be in the cottage in the first place?

As he shuffled down the snow-covered pathway, neither did he notice Detective Inspector Riley's police car.

"You'll catch your death out here without a coat, what are you doing?"

The unexpected sound of the man's voice caught Ant by surprise. At first, he didn't answer. Instead, he alternated his attention between his police friend and the diamond.

Holding the precious object between forefinger and thumb, he held the glistening stone out in front of him.

"It's a beautiful thing, Peter, don't you think?"

The inspector stepped forward, taking care not to slip in the treacherous conditions. "Is that what I think it is?"

"It is." Anthony pivoted the exquisite gem from side to

side, causing light to bounce off its precisely cut surface in all directions.

"From inside the cottage?"

"I know what you're thinking."

"You mean your family paid it's head gardener so much he could afford diamonds, or there's a more sinister explanation. Let's get you inside before you freeze and so we can have a good look at the diamond."

Although Stanton Hall was cold most of the year, the difference in temperature between its snow-covered grounds and the festivities inside provided welcome relief for its shivering son and heir.

"Where is the other half of you?" asked Peter Riley as the pair gathered around the Aga in the deserted kitchen.

"Don't you start, I've already had that line from Fitch." Ant held his hands close to one hotplate and massaged his fingers to make the most of the radiated heat.

"Please yourself, I'll put it down to your brain being as chilled as those fingers. Anyway, let's have a good look at the diamond."

Calm down, Anthony, Percy's disappearance isn't his fault.

"It's a beautiful thing, isn't it?"

"It sure is, let me have a proper look." Riley retrieved the precious object from his companion's chilled fingers and held it up to the light. Its faceted surfaces beamed shards of bright light around the white-tiled surfaces of the kitchen.

"Beautiful it may be, Peter, but it makes no sense for the thing to have been in that cottage."

Riley gave the stone a final admiring glance before handing it back to his host. "Then, we agree. It's almost certain your uncle's disappearance, and the discovery of that thing is no coincidence." He pointed at the glistening diamond as Anthony wrapped it in a paper tissue and placed it deep into his trouser pocket.

"There's something I need to tell you."

"Jake Bateman?"

Riley nodded. "One of my patrols saw him disappearing into the woods about a mile from here. You know what that means."

"Are you sure?"

"As sure as we can be. However, you and I both know we can't afford to take a risk." Riley pulled back his coat sleeve and flicked his wrist to reveal a wafer-thin watch. "We have approximately ninety minutes before Bateman's deadline expires. I'm as inclined as you to believe the man's a crank, but the fact he is making his way back to the Hall gives me considerable cause for concern."

Anthony made his way to the back door. "I'll take the Land Rover; can you get more officers over here?"

"Hang on a minute. Land Rover, what are you talking about? Where do you expect to look?"

Dammit, the man has a point.

"We can't just stand here and—"

"And what? I'm not suggesting for a minute we act like lame ducks and wait for the man to do his worst. That said, we need to be methodical and stay calm.

"I've already ordered backup and my men will work their way outwards from the Hall and into the woods. I have other officers stationed on the road in case he gets jittery and makes a run for it. He won't succeed a second time, I promise you."

How did I misjudge you so grievously in the past?

The two men exchanged penetrating glances, each giving a single nod to show mutual respect.

"Let me at least gather some volunteers to help search the grounds."

Riley broke into a smile. "Of course. The more eyes we have on the ground, the more likely we are to catch this braggart."

————

"Did you say you found it in the cottage?" The earl scrutinised the glittering diamond as he held it in front of the open fire in the library. "It's quite something isn't it, Son."

"What I cannot fathom is how long it lay there. Even though the cottage is often empty, it defies logic that it could have been there so long without being discovered. Put that together with the blood Lyn and I found in the same room. Well, it doesn't bear thinking about."

The Earl of Stanton rose slowly from his chair and walked to a set of library steps.

"What are you doing, can I help?"

The elderly gentleman brushed his son's concern aside. "I'm not in my dotage, at least not yet. Let's worry about how the diamond got there in a few minutes. For now, we should concentrate on how old it is."

"Why should that matter?"

"You're slipping, Anthony. If this is a modern diamond, its presence in the cottage offers one scenario. If it's old, well, that could mean something quite different. Help me down, Son."

One of these days you'll push yourself too far, Father.

Thankful to get his father safely back into his favourite chair, Anthony watched as the earl thumbed an old reference book.

After what seemed like an age to the son, his father

pointed to a monochrome image. "I thought so. This diamond dates back to the Middle Ages."

Anthony frowned. "How do you know that?"

The earl pointed to a half-page, black-and-white image. "Unless I'm mistaken, this beautiful creature is heart cut. According to the notes here, in the sixteenth century.

"However, because of the expense of creating the cut, only the rich could afford its romantic shape. In fact, it says here that Mary Queen of Scots owned such diamonds and gave one to her cousin, Elizabeth the First in fifteen sixty-two."

"You're joking, look what happened to her. And they say diamonds are a girl's best friend."

His father smiled. "You are naughty, my darling. It poses at least one intriguing question."

"You mean, who it belongs to?"

The earl shook his head, closed the reference book, and looked at his son. "I think it would be more accurate to use the past tense. These are completely out of fashion today because we much prefer the modern oval- or radiant-cut diamonds."

Anthony took the diamond from his father to survey its glistening surfaces. "I may have misunderstood. Are you saying this links with Stanton Hall's past?

"In a word, yes, although it does not form part of our family's collection. I can check the archives, but I'm almost certain I won't find any reference to it."

"How can you be so sure, Father?"

"Because although we won the Hall and estate on the turn of a card, the family was in all other respects, of modest means. There isn't any way they could have afforded such an object."

That means only one thing.

"Are you suggesting there's a hoard that belonged to the original owners of the Hall hidden somewhere?"

"If we follow that scenario to its logical conclusion, the more pressing question is, who found it and what do they intend to do?

———

"THANK YOU FOR VOLUNTEERING, EVERYONE. I ASK ONLY ONE thing, and that is you don't put yourself in danger. We don't know whether Bateman is a fool, or a cold killer."

Anthony stood on the third step of the grand staircase in the hallway as he addressed upwards of a dozen men and women who'd willingly agreed to help the police search the grounds.

Fitch joined his friend on the stairs. "I've done my best to describe this idiot to you and please, don't be fooled if you come across a man who appears to be drunk. Bateman may well be off his head with alcohol, or it may be an act. Either way, don't take any chances."

In seconds the ragtag volunteers stood under the portico of the Hall's entrance awaiting instructions from Detective Inspector Riley, surrounded by police officers huddled in the snow a few feet away.

"Please pair yourself with one of my officers who will take the lead in guiding you as we get going. We shall begin by standing approximately twenty feet apart and proceed in a line into the woods. If you see anything, tell my officer and they will radio me."

Within a minute they were off, the only sound scrunching snow, as each made their way through the crisp whiteness towards the blackness of ten thousand trees.

"Thanks for getting the message out, Fitch. I can't tell you how grateful I am."

The mechanic grinned as he bumped into his oldest friend, almost making the man fall into a snowdrift. "That's what mates are for, my friend. But to be honest, the only thing that's puzzling me is where Lyn is. I can't find her anywhere."

"It's funny you should say that; I've been so wrapped up in other things that I had lost track of time. Perhaps Lyn is with my mother. Anyway, she's safe inside, that's the chief thing."

Fitch nodded as his friend brought him up to date about the diamond and his discussion with the earl. "Blimey, this is turning into a good old mystery. A madman on the loose, a missing uncle and an old gem worth a fortune. I tell you what, your family know how to make Christmas go off with a bang, that's for sure."

Now, deep in the woods, there was utter silence. The quietness that came with the deep snowfall was made more intense by the thick canopy of elm and majestic oak trees.

"There he is!" The excited declaration caused police radios to crackle to life as each officer attempted to confirm who had made the sighting. The pace of events moved from a slow, methodical search to one of confusion as a search party splintered to track down their quarry.

Detective Inspector Riley immediately got a grip on the situation. "Maintain radio silence, maintain radio silence. Hold your positions. No one is to speak unless it's to inform me of relevant information. You will all then listen to my commands. Do you all understand?"

A steady trickle of confirmations followed.

"I want the officer who saw the man to confirm that to me now." Silence fell until his radio clicked a few seconds later. "PC 214, boss. I saw him run from behind a large oak, twenty feet in front of me. I believe I'm approximately fifty feet east of you, sir."

"All officers, close ranks; move to the tree line, now."

Anthony adjusted the volume on the police radio Riley had lent him as he led Fitch to the rendezvous point.

That's how to use power.

Bateman was still one step ahead of them. As the police and volunteers reached open ground, a figure ran towards the old stables.

"There he goes," shouted Riley as he urged his officers on. "Williams, you still in the hallway?"

Riley's radio clicked as it readied itself to receive a call. "Affirmative, sir."

"Move to the main kitchens immediately. You'll have full view of the stable. Do not, repeat, do not exit the premises. Eyes only."

"Affirmative and out."

The progress of the combined police and volunteer force slowed as large flakes of snow driven on by a strengthening breeze slammed into their faces.

Riley once again flicked his radio to life. Do not enter the stable yard, repeat, do not enter. I don't want the snow disturbed. "

Within two minutes, the search party congregated as per the detective's instructions.

"Where is he?" mused Riley as he scanned the empty space.

Anthony joined the inspector to offer what advice he could. "It looks as though plenty of people, including me, trampled all over the yard, so this is not going to be easy."

"I agree; then again, I think the newly fallen snow is our friend."

"What do you mean?"

Riley pointed to a pattern of footprints. "He's a clever one, given that. Bateman hasn't headed straight for the nearest door. Riley tried to crouch down. Can you see those footprints are deeper than the others?"

Anthony joined Riley on his haunches and followed the detective's pointing finger. "You're right, Peter. Bateman is the last person to cross this area, so the snow hasn't had time to fill his tracks."

Both men suddenly noticed a man frantically waving from the kitchen window.

"It's Williams—he's spotted our man."

Anthony turned to look at the window to see the police constable pointing to the far corner of the stable yard.

"He's pointing to the tack room. We need to get in quickly because that room gives direct access to an old staff corridor. If he gets through that, he could disappear in seconds."

Riley turned to his men. "You two follow me. All other officers wait here in case he makes a break for it. Volunteers, thank you for your help; I suggest you now get inside and warm yourselves up. Please say nothing to the other guests, we don't want to cause undue alarm."

Fitch disregarded the inspector's instructions, instead joining the advance party as they slowly crossed the stable yard and neared the tack-room door.

"Quietly does it now, people. Ready? Strike, strike, strike."

This reminds me of active service.

In a split second, all five rushed through the iron-studded door and into the spacious workroom. Fitch flicked on the light switch, which momentarily illuminated the room before its old bulb failed.

Two police officers immediately produced their standard-issue torches and scanned every surface of the bedraggled space.

Riley had a finger up to his lips to signify quiet as he gestured for the other four to close in around him. "Working in pairs, open every door, check every nook and cranny. I'll watch the door in case he attempts to make a break for it."

Ant and Fitch peeled off to the left while the two police constables went right. Seconds seemed like hours as they methodically cleared the room. As Fitch opened a storeroom door, he shot backwards and fell awkwardly on the red-tiled floor.

"It's him," shouted Anthony as the man barged past him and made for the door.

Peter Riley was ready for him and stopped Bateman by extending his leg, causing the intruder to tumble forward and fall into the deep snow of the stable yard.

"Good job, Peter."

"I call that move my 'gotcha.' It saves all that effort of running after villains and wrestling them to the ground. You two, get that idiot to his feet and cuff him."

"Don't mind me, I'll be all right." Fitch's obtuse plea for help fell on deaf ears as everyone else hurried out to make sure Bateman did not escape again.

Bundling the prisoner across the stable yard and into the warmth of the kitchen took less than a minute. "Sit him down and keep a hand on each shoulder. I don't want him going anywhere."

"Yes boss," replied the two constables as they took up their positions.

Riley allowed the room to fall into silence. Bateman's gaze dropped to the floor as the detective pulled up a chair and sat directly in front of his prisoner.

Meanwhile, Anthony and Fitch stood behind the inspector, arms folded tightly across their chests, making them a menacing sight.

"Why have you come here tonight?" Riley's question met with silence. "I'll ask you one more time before I put you back outside to think things over, or let you freeze. Why did you come to Stanton Hall this evening?"

Bateman shot Riley a vicious look. "I came for the Christmas party. Why are you here?"

Anthony's blood boiled. He moved forward, stopped only by Riley's outstretched arm.

"We'll not do it that way."

Bateman smirked.

"Just to clarify, freezing to death doesn't leave any marks, Mr Bateman."

The prisoner's self-satisfied smirk vanished in an instant. "You wouldn't dare."

Detective Inspector Riley sat forward so that his face was only two feet from Bateman's. "Is that a risk you're prepared to take? You should know that I am. After all, who will contradict what I tell the police's Department of Internal Affairs? Not you, that's for certain. Now, you said someone at the Hall would die by midnight. That's less than sixty minutes away. Talk now, or I put you in the yard?"

Bateman scowled at the inspector, then repeated his smirk. "Yes, I told you, somebody will be dead by midnight. The only thing you don't know is who will die, do you?"

Anthony lurched forward, this time undeterred by Peter Riley's attempt to stop him. He grabbed Bateman's collar and shook him. "Tell me what you know, or I'll not be responsible for my actions. I know you worked with my father, so you'll probably have been told about my background.

"Believe me, Mr Bateman, you do not want to experience the other Anthony Stanton. Do you understand me?"

Fitch moved forward and touched his friend on the shoulder. Anthony immediately let go of Bateman while maintaining eye contact as he stepped back.

"Leave it, Ant. He's not worth it."

Undeterred, he continued to glare at Bateman.

Riley flicked his finger to show that his officers should lift Bateman to his feet. "Cuff him to the hand pump in the middle of the yard. Let's see what half an hour in the snow does to his memory."

The two officers hesitated as they exchanged alarmed looks.

Riley stood up. "Get on with it, then. Out he goes."

The officers dragged the unwilling prisoner towards the back door. "All right, all right. I'll talk."

The detective signalled for his officers to put Bateman back into his chair. "It's so good of you to help with police enquiries. Now, talk."

The man glared at Anthony. "He and his father think they can do what they want with people just because they're rich and own land. I've worked hard since coming here, and they just toss me out with no notice. No job, no house, no nothing."

Peter Riley turned to Anthony who was shaking his head, an action which incensed Bateman even more.

"I hate your sort. We're expected to bow and scrape; Yes sir, no sir, three bags full, sir. You act as if it's the Middle Ages and we are mere chattels you can buy and sell at will. Well you can't; I turned the tables so you were the frightened ones. It worked, didn't it?"

Anthony walked to the table and leant against its edge. He was less than three feet from Bateman. "So, the fact you stole from your employer had nothing to do with being let go? I've done some checking up on you over the last few hours, Mr Bateman.

"It seems your manager was less than impressed with your bullying attitude, and light-fingered habits. Do you know you almost caused one of my staff to have a nasty accident when you removed the safety guard from the table saw?

Bateman shrugged his shoulders. "He had it coming to him, looking at me as if I was a piece of rubbish. No one does that to me. Especially not your type."

Peter Riley ambled over to his friend and spoke in a low voice. "This bloke has a persecution complex, Anthony. But I don't think it goes any further than that. If you ask me, he just got lucky your relative went missing on the day he played his little game."

"What if you're wrong, Peter? There are several hundred people in this building at the moment. In thirty minutes we may have one less. I ask again, Peter, what if you've got this wrong?"

Just then, Fitch's mobile rang. "Sorry, can you say that again? You sound as if you're swimming underwater... have you nothing better to do this late on a Christmas Eve? What, no... That makes little sense. Are you sure?"

"That sounded odd. Is everything okay?" asked Anthony as Fitch ended the call.

"No, mate, things are far from okay. That was my mate who did me a favour by lifting those two cars this morning."

"And?"

"It's routine they check vehicle details when they recover vehicles from the crash site. In particular, who owns what."

"Sorry, I'm not following."

"Dr Thorndike's car checked out. It's registered to him, and everything else is in order."

"Fitch, I sense you're about to say 'but'?"

The mechanic gave Ant a long, hard stare. "Spot on, mate. The other car is registered to your Uncle Percy."

Anthony reeled. "Fitch, I need you to check something for me, and time is about to run out."

The electrifying atmosphere of the kitchen reached a new level as an internal door opened.

"Lyn, where have you been—are you okay?"

"Never mind about that now, Ant. I need to talk to you."

16

11:07 P.M. CHRISTMAS EVE

Excitement grew in the great hall as the cheerful villagers began clock watching. Tradition called for the lights to dim at eleven forty-five, which signalled the beginning of a much-loved communal act.

Meanwhile, senior members of the extended Stanton family, together with one or two other specially invited guests gathered in the morning room.

"You sure you want to do this in front of the family?"

Anthony nodded at Detective Inspector Riley. "If in the next fifteen minutes, I cannot show the need to heal wounds, this family is lost."

The two men walked with purpose in their stride as they moved from the library to address the guests. As agreed, David, the butler, stood sentinel outside the ornately panelled door to the morning room.

"Did you get them all?" His tone was polite but determined.

"As you asked, sir, though one or two showed some reluctance."

"I'm sure they did, David. Okay, let's get on with it."

The butler pulled the cuffs of his white gloves before turning a large brass doorknob and easing the door open. The low hubbub that emanated from the room a few seconds earlier stopped immediately as they caught sight of their hosts.

In the few seconds he had before making his address, Anthony made a point of engaging each person with a piercing stare. Some he knew well, other family members more distantly.

Behind him, the butler quietly closed the door, effectively isolating the gathering from the villagers and the celebrations.

"This is the second time today you have instructed us to gather. What is going on, Nephew? It really won't do!"

Standing to the side of the great Adams fireplace, Anthony looked to his questioner without smiling. "I know my request may appear odd, Aunt May, but I wanted to get you all together to bring closure to what has been an extraordinary day."

"And your private little family get-together requires a detective inspector and several people whom I have never met before?"

"Yes, Uncle Cedric." Ant turned to Riley. The two men's eyes met. "My friend is here both in a personal and professional capacity, more of which later."

The room's attention moved towards the door as it slowly opened. "The Earl and Lady Stanton." The butler stepped aside to allow his employers to enter the room before closing the door behind them. Several older members of the family instinctively rose to their feet in deference to the head of the family and his wife. They remained standing until Anthony's mother and father took their seats.

"Sorry we're late, Son. So many villagers wanting to wish us a happy Christmas. How lucky we are to know such people."

Quite a contrast with what's going on in here.

Anthony gave his parents an affectionate smile. "We are. In fact," he continued as he turned to face his audience, "you could say that's one outcome I hope for over the next few minutes. "

That's foxed them.

"But for the next few minutes, I want you to listen to Detective Inspector Riley. He has one or two matters to share, and perhaps a few questions to ask."

Riley moved from his friend to take up a position on the opposite side of the fireplace. The only sound making its presence felt as he walked across a deep-carpet pile was spitting embers, making their escape up the chimney.

"This is looking like a game of charades."

Riley smiled. "Forgive me for not knowing your name, and we have no time to make individual introductions this evening, but you make a point. In fact, you might say today has played out like a game. Except this game was deadly."

Anthony picked up on the theme. "Cousin William, today's events call into question what and who we are as a family. Also, how others view us. It would be easy to brush several things off as mere coincidences but—"

"As a police officer," interrupted Riley, "I don't believe in such things."

I love this. They don't know which one of us to look at.

Anthony looked across to Peter Riley and gestured for him to continue.

"Christmas is a wonderful time, isn't it? You know we all come together, offer each other season's greetings and attempt to be in a good mood. To be tolerant of others. The problem is, and I'm afraid it's something I deal with every day of my working life, there are people driven by greed, loathing, even envy."

"Present company excepted, of course," interjected Anthony.

"Indeed," replied Riley, "or at least as far as most people in this room are concerned."

The detective's stinging remark reverberated around the spacious room as a short-lived hubbub filled the air.

"Between around ten o'clock last night and ten thirty this morning, Uncle Percy disappeared."

May sprang to her feet to challenge her nephew. "You imply a malign force is in play. There is no evidence that stupid man disappeared for any other reason than his usual selfishness."

Several shouts of "hear, hear" emanated from the gathering.

Riley held a finger up as if about to ask a quick question. "Let us just suppose for one minute that was the case. The question we must next ask is, why? Having arrived at the Hall just a few hours earlier, why disappear without displaying the courtesy to inform his host?"

May once more sprang to her feet. "Because he is a deceitful, detestable man."

Guests shifted uncomfortably on the chairs.

"If I may continue." The room fell into silence, such was the authority in the detective's tone. "Be careful what you say, and how you say it. Remember that I am, foremost, a police officer. Some might take your outburst as an admission of guilt."

The room broke into an uproar of shouting and finger pointing. In the middle of the maelstrom sat May, her cheeks purple with rage.

An intervention came from an unexpected quarter in the form of the earl. Rising from his chair, he did not speak or make any other gesture. Instead, he stood bolt upright, which showed his austere upbringing and military career.

It took only a few seconds for the crowd to realise the Earl of Stanton was on his feet, demanding the respect due to him.

"You are in my house. You'll pay my son and Inspector Riley the courtesy of listening to what they have to say. That is how we shall proceed."

The earl's quiet yet commanding words had the desired effect.

"Anthony, perhaps you would like to take up the story?" said Riley.

"Thank you, Inspector." The two men exchanged nods. "Aunt May, we now know that Percy had, over recent years, taken against travelling in wet or dangerous conditions. When he made the journey to the Hall yesterday, although the weather was cold, you'll recall it was dry. By lunchtime today snow was falling, so even if he had driven away earlier. He'd not have continued his journey when the weather deteriorated and would've contacted us."

Cedric made his presence known. "You assume he was in a fit state to make such a call?"

Anthony stepped forward a few paces. "Yes, Uncle Cedric, your assumption is correct. However, as we shall see, there is a danger of making two plus two equal five if we believe our own prejudices. I—"

"I must protest. You're talking about my brother. I think I know him better than you. I speak from a lifetime of experience of picking up the pieces left by my eccentric sibling. I won't have you insinuating anything to the contrary. Instead of this theatre of mystery, you're forcing the family to enjoy, your police friend and you might, perhaps, put more effort into finding Percy. If you don't, we shall."

This is going well.

"I make no judgement on your relationship with Percy, Uncle Cedric; instead, I point the finger at myself. I, too, at first assumed your brother had, for some mysterious reason known only to himself, left the Hall." Anthony looked across to Riley.

"And I understand why Lord Stanton came to that conclusion. Let us consider the evidence. A member of your family stays in a tiny cottage rather than in the comfort of this noble house, with a bed covered in detailed building plans of Stanton Hall and a concealed patch of blood in the living room.

"As the detective, I'm presented with two scenarios. The first is that of Percy Stanton receiving an injury of some sort by means unknown. He panics and drives to the nearest hospital, yet the weather deteriorates so he must stop."

"My officers have been out in their patrol cars since the snow fell. Despite the foul weather, with one exception, there have been only minor bumps and scrapes and, thankfully, no serious injuries. The second scenario suggests that the gentleman never left this estate.

"This, of course, triggers the question: where is he? Several of the earl's staff, my officers, and several volunteers have carried out extensive searches of the grounds, finding nothing."

Anthony picked up on the detective's thread. "That is apart from three sightings of a figure dressed from head to toe in purple, oh, yes, and a gentleman who prophesied one of us will die within the next thirty-five minutes."

———

In parallel to Anthony's family meeting, Lyn and Fitch were deep in conversation as they sat in one of the estate Land Rovers outside the old head gardener's cottage.

"Are you sure you want to do this, Lyn? Haven't you been through enough today?"

"I know you're looking out for me, Fitch, but Anthony wants to bring the family back together. If it means doing this, I'm prepared to. What about you, will there be enough time?"

Fitch took out his mobile and scanned the digital clock on his home screen. "It will be tight, but Stu started out a while ago, so with luck, he should make the rendezvous."

Lyn glanced at her wristwatch. "If this snow continues to fall heavily, do you think the roads will stay open?"

Fitch wiped the windscreen with the back of his gloved hand to look at the near whiteout conditions. "If that tank he drives can't get through, then nothing will. Whether this Land Rover can manage is quite another matter, but I've got to give it my best shot."

As if on cue, Fitch's mobile rang. "Great, how's the weather your end? Yes, much the same here... Okay, see you in fifteen."

"That sounded promising?"

Fitch took a second look at the snowstorm swirling around the vehicle. "He's almost there, so fingers crossed I can get to him. Listen, good luck, and don't take any unnecessary risks."

Lyn leant over and placed a sisterly kiss on her friend's cheek. "And the same to you. Right, I'm off; you'd better get going."

Within seconds of Lyn clambering out of the snow-covered vehicle, Fitch had turned it around. He engaged the four-wheel drive and moved off, crunching the build-up of snow beneath its wheels with determination.

Lyn turned to face the cottage as the Land Rover's rear lights faded into the wintry distance. She fixed her eyes on a figure at the front corner of the house.

She's waiting for me.

Lyn struggled to move forward through a deep drift that had built up around the open garden gate. A whiteout momentarily blinded her as she doggedly pushed through the icy mound. Brushing her collar, she saw the figure looking back at her as it moved to the back corner of the cottage.

I know where you're leading me.

Trudging doggedly through a thick layer of virgin snow, it didn't phase Lyn that the figure left a trail. On she went, leaving the cottage behind until she stood in the old pigsty.

Sleep well, I know I'll see you again.

Forging through a second deep drift that had piled against the small covered space Lyn had found a scrap of red fabric in, she was thankful to be out of the chill wind and falling snow.

Now I understand where the draft came from when I searched here with Ant.

Taking a small torch from her heavy winter coat, Lyn shone its narrow beam across the stone floor.

Got you.

She cleared several wind-driven frosted leaves and a small amount of accumulated snow from the far corner of the small space. Lyn traced a gloved hand along the joint between a square stone flag approximately fourteen inches across from its neighbours. She knew someone had moved it because of an absence of dusty debris where it abutted the other floor slabs.

Let's see whether Dr Philpott is correct.

Illuminating two small sections of wall starting from the corner, Lyn pressed each brick. The task took several minutes. She was about to abandon her efforts, when one brick she touched moved a fraction of an inch.

Good heavens, he was right.

Lyn heard the distinctive click as she pressed the brick harder. To her delight, the stone slab she thought suspicious flicked up on its front edge just enough for her to get her fingers underneath it.

Wow, this is heavy.

As she raised the stone inch by inch, it pivoted back until it rested against a brick wall behind it. Lyn immediately felt a rush of air blowing into her face.

That's clever.

Peering into the blackness, Lyn shone her torch downwards. She could just make out a brick-weave floor about four feet down.

I hope the creepy crawlies are all hibernating.

A moment's hesitation passed as Lyn sat on the edge of the small opening, her legs dangling into the abyss. Using her arms for support, she eased herself through the entrance and closed her eyes.

Please let me not break anything when I land.

Feeling pleased with herself that she landed on her feet, she soon realised that without a small torch, she wouldn't be able to see one foot being placed in front of the other.

Even when she switched the torch on, it took several seconds to adjust to the dank and forbidding conditions she now found herself in.

How did he do this on his own?

Crouching so she could clear the entrance, Lyn soon realised it was impossible to stand upright.

Nothing for it but to get on all fours.

Inching forward, it felt to Lyn as if it were taking an age to cover even a few yards. A few minutes later, she rested against a brick side of the narrow tunnel. She shone a torch ahead and noticed something glistening.

That's odd. What's broken glass doing down here?

Crawling forward until she was in touching distance of the object, she couldn't believe what she was looking at.

It's a diamond. This is crazy.

Lyn shone a torch excitedly backwards and forwards to cover as much ground in as little time as she could. As a beam of light caught a section of wall to her left, she noticed a deep scratch in the soft brickwork and ran her finger down its short length.

It's clean, so it's new. Very odd?

Lyn tucked the precious stone into her pocket and continued to crawl along the dismal tunnel, which seemed to have no end. As she continued, she heard a faint noise in the distance.

I must be imagining things. Then again, if Philpott is right...

As she continued to move forward, the tunnel widened, also the cold draft she'd been aware of since lifting the entrance stone intensified.

Someone is down here.

The noise she'd heard a little earlier identified itself. It wasn't the draft causing debris to scratch against the tunnel's ancient walls.

Oh, no.

"HELLO, MATE, I OWE YOU ONE COMING ALL THIS WAY ON Christmas Eve, never mind the weather." Fitch gave his friend a firm handshake as they smiled at each other, blinking almost continuously to clear the falling snowflakes from their eyes.

"You know I love being out in the foul weather, Fitch. Anyway, the wife's chuffed to get me out from under her feet. She says I keep interfering when she's getting presents ready for the kids. I don't have a clue what she's talking about."

Fitch let out a belly laugh as he followed his friend back to the recovery truck, jumping in to escape the worst of the weather. "What was that story you told me once about burning one of your lad's slot car engines out before he even got to use it on Christmas day?"

"I can always go home again, you know. Do you want this or not? Anyway, June agreed that I should put the track up for the lad. Is it my fault the car burst into flames after just a couple of hours racing?"

Fitch raised his eyebrows and shook his head. "Perhaps I'll ask your June when I see her, shall I?"

The two friends laughed as they reminisced about past adventures on the road.

"Is it still in the car? You haven't touched it, have you?"

"Yes, it is, and no, I haven't. Do you think I'm daft or something?"

Fitch reached into a small plastic bag he brought with him. "Good lad, fancy a mince pie?"

His friend's eyes widened. "Top man, I'll have two."

Fitch reached back into the bag and retrieved a second Christmas treat. "I guess that's the least I can do. What say we have a quick look at it before you follow me back to Stanton Hall?"

Taking a huge bite out of a mince pie, the friend frowned. "What, go back outside in this. Are you mad or something?"

Fitch brushed bits of pastry from his chest that had flown out of his friend's mouth. "Weren't you taught not to talk with your mouth full? Then again, why change the habit of a lifetime."

His friend gave a toothy grin before downing the rest of the pie.

After a spell of shaking his head, the man opened the driver's door as Fitch followed suit. Both took a sharp intake of breath as the cold air and avalanche of falling snow hit them.

The things you get me to do, Anthony Stanton. I must be mad.

Each brushed the snow off a rear door handle to gain entrance to the damaged vehicle. Now partially shielded from the inclement weather, Fitch's gaze concentrated on a shiny object cocooned in a thick woollen scarf.

"You reckon they killed somebody for this, do you?"

Fitch gave his friend a wistful look. "Lyn is checking that now. I just hope we're wrong. Either way, we need to get this back pronto so we can get Inspector Riley to look at it."

"Then you'd better lead on, Macduff. I'll get you a two-way radio from the cab, so we can keep in touch, yes?"

"That's a great idea, mate."

Shortly after, Fitch fired up his Land Rover, then turned on the vehicle's main beam and windscreen wipers before setting off for Stanton Hall. In his rear-view mirror, he could see the flashing orange lights of his friend's recovery vehicle refracting off the falling snow as if it were a Christmas tree.

The conditions are getting worse. Ten more minutes and we're safe.

"Sharp right turn coming up, mate; make sure you keep moving and watch out for the drainage ditch on your left, it's quite a narrow track."

In his haste to get out of the recovery vehicle's way, Fitch caused the Land Rover to drift to the left as he turned off the main road.

Don't say I'm going to end up in the stupid ditch. He'll never let me live it down.

"You okay, Fitch? Be careful there, buddy. Coming through now."

"I'm through, mate. You're clear."

Thank heavens for that. Now let's get up to the Hall.

———

BACK IN THE MORNING ROOM, DETECTIVE INSPECTOR RILEY and Anthony continued to hold court over the guests.

"Fortunately, thanks to a joint effort between the Inspector's men and several villagers, we have apprehended the suspect. The good news is he's in handcuffs and has the company of two constables in the kitchen. Not so good news is that we don't know if his threats are a hoax, he's working with somebody else inside the Hall, or he's laid some kind of surprise for us."

Once again, May got to her feet. "Are you suggesting one of us is in league with whoever this fellow is? If that is the case, Nephew, they would want out of this little get-together, don't you think?"

Inspector Riley took the lead in responding. "Madam, that is the second time you have incriminated yourself. It seems you have a simple idea of what his accomplice, if he has one, will and won't do. I strongly urge you to calm down, unless that is, there is something you wish to tell me?"

The room once more erupted into an uproar. This time the Earl of Stanton did not quell the agitated gathering.

"There is a great deal of difference between disliking someone and killing them or arranging for the person to die. Your assertions are preposterous, and if this is how Her Majesty's police force goes about its business, it's no wonder the force's conviction rates are so appalling."

Don't let her intimidate you, Peter.

Anthony couldn't tell what the detective thought; what he saw was his calm exterior.

"I'm more concerned, madam, with Mr Percival Stanton's absence, not your views on the police service. Please, sit down."

May stood her ground for a few seconds before slowly resuming her seat while keeping her eyes fixed on the detective inspector.

The butler broke the awkward atmosphere by once again discreetly opening the panelled door. Fitch entered the room but said nothing. Looking across to Anthony, he nodded once before leaving the room.

"Well, that's one more piece of the puzzle that has fallen into place. Soon the game will be up. The question is, why did this happen, and what are we to do?" Anthony held an open hand out to Riley, who accepted the invitation to speak.

"Murder is a dreadful thing. However, what has always appalled me is that the victim often knew their assailant. Astonishingly, so many murdered people die with a surprised look on their face.

"This brings me to the matter in hand. Mr Cedric Stanton, if I may have your attention." Heads turned, and eyes widened to focus on the man, who sat nervously. "You had every reason to kill your brother. You have made it quite clear today how much you resented your sibling until you grew up.

"You confessed to detesting having to 'clear up the mess after him.' Also, there is no doubt in my mind you continue to hold him responsible for fracturing the family's cohesion."

Lord Stanton's authoritative voice floated around the room. "Can this be true, Cedric?" The elderly gentleman's voice betrayed no emotion as he spoke.

Cedric shook his head without responding. Ant noticed his nose twitching and his hands curled into fists so tight that the taut skin had drained of colour.

"Murdering someone, despite what you see on fictional TV programmes, is not a simple thing to do. A family dispute that's festered and conflated with other issues can rapidly deteriorate into a situation where one or both parties descend into primaeval violence. Some killers describe it as 'a red mist descending.' Is that what happened, Cedric?"

Cedric sprang to his feet and hurried towards the door. "I've had enough of this. Your accusations are groundless, egregious and offensive. I'll not put up with this nonsense any longer."

As he reached the door, Anthony called out to him. "We believe you, Uncle. There is no doubt you have good reason to dislike your brother. But then, that is something most siblings experience. Please take your seat. However, if you prefer to be somewhere else, that is up to you. No one will stop you."

His nephew's words caused Cedric to stop dead, his hand still on the brass doorknob. The two men exchanged grim eye contact until Anthony's uncle retracted his hand and walked silently back to his seat. It was possible to hear a pin drop in the electrifying atmosphere of the morning room.

"That brings me to you, Miss May Stanton." Riley spoke softly as he addressed the irritated woman. "It seems you, above all others, have a motive for killing Percival Stanton. Using your own words, you have condemned him as the man who wrecked your happiness.

"Having the love of your life snatched away from you has the power to send people mad. It drives others to kill, sometimes decades after the event, just like you killed Percival."

The room descended into a chaotic jumble of whispered conversations, pointing fingers. In the middle of it all, May sat motionless, her eyes downcast.

As the room waited for her to respond, Anthony wandered over to the Inspector and whispered into his ear. Riley nodded and left the room.

"Now that the Inspector has left, perhaps you might tell us what happened, May.

His aunt slowly rose and instead of looking at her interrogator, fixed her gaze on the earl. "I spoke to Percy by telephone last night. We had a terrible argument, and I warned him he hadn't heard the last of it by a long shot.

"He was his usual selfish self and attempted to dismiss me as if I were one of his undergraduates. I made it clear I would have none of it and that when we met, there would be a reckoning."

May fell quiet, allowing Anthony to press harder without the need to interrupt his relative. "And when you came across each other?"

"We didn't. Believe you me, had I seen him, there would've been trouble. Yes, I confess as much. However, after we spoke by phone, I had no further contact with him.

"Frankly, if he has come to a sticky end, the rest of you

will experience the sense of loss and hopelessness that I have experienced for so long. To be honest, his disappearance gives me a sense of closure. How the rest of you interpret that, I cannot judge."

As May resumed her seat and folded her hands across her lap, Detective Inspector Riley re-entered the room. He carried a cardboard box measuring approximately twelve inches square.

"Have I missed anything, Anthony?"

The earl's son shook his head without speaking.

"That just leaves you, Dr Philpott."

The occupants of the room looked at one another before turning to the far end of the room.

"What... what nonsense is this?"

"You said that you called in at the Hall because you were concerned about Percy. Why didn't you just ring?"

In the distance, the wailing of an ambulance disturbed the uncanny silence of the room as all present awaited Philpott's response.

"I told you, Percy is a close colleague and dear friend. His telephone call to me was disturbing and out of character. I felt compelled to visit and check that all was well."

Peter Riley took up the questioning. "Are you colleagues or competitors? Academics have a track record in stealing each other's research so they can publish under their own name and collect the plaudits. In fact, I'm told you're a rather selfish lot. Isn't that so?"

Philpott stood to plead his innocence. He shrugged his shoulders. "Look, yes, I suppose to outsiders we are a strange lot. We are used to accusations of being eccentric grey-haired old men in our ivory towers. What some don't understand is the science that we produce, the technology used for good all around the world.

"In my own field of expertise, this extends to the discoveries we make, which tells us who we were, and how it shapes what we are. Yes, there is professional rivalry and jealousy. We all strive for excellence. But it doesn't mean we murder each other. I say again, Percy is someone I'm honoured to call a friend."

Riley narrowed his eyes as he made the gathering wait for his next question. "I think it was an accident. You had no intention of harming Percy when you found out what he had discovered. Something of such importance that it would make your career.

"I'm sure you try your best to apply the logical argument that he should share the glory with you. Not least, you had a long history of shared research. But he refused, didn't he, and an argument ensued, and you hit him? The question is, Dr Philpott, where is he. At least allow the family to recover his body."

Philpott put his head in his hands and wept. "It's true, I was jealous. He was such an excellent researcher; his method and attention to detail were faultless. I pleaded with him when we spoke to share what he had discovered, but he refused. He said his discovery will right a great wrong."

Riley pressed his argument. "He agreed to meet you, didn't he? When you met, you argued, and you killed him."

A communal gasp filled the room.

"No, I did not."

Riley's tone softened. "I believe you."

A second gasp permeated the room. Philpott slowly raised his head. "You mean..."

"We checked your phone records. The timings were as you suggested. There is no evidence that you left your premises, or that you met Percival Stanton. Whether you came to do harm is quite another matter and of no consequence now, since the man had already disappeared by the time you arrived.

"However, it was important that I tested your alibi. It might surprise you to know how often people attempt to deceive the police. Please take your seat."

Philpott collapsed into his chair before putting his head in his hands again.

A voice from the middle of the room drew everyone's attention. "Is that it, or have you another little trick to play before we can enjoy our Christmas?"

Anthony grinned. "It's interesting you should say that cousin. I have one last, do you know I was going to say 'rabbit to pull out my hat'? In fact, it's more accurate to say, one more lady to appear as if from nowhere."

Riley crossed in front of the grand fireplace to stand at his friend's side.

"Are you going to do the honours?"

"You're the guest in this house, Peter; I think the honour should be yours."

Riley stepped towards the wall next to the fireplace covered with rich oak panelling. He extended his left hand to what looked like a knot in the panel framing and depressed it while using his right hand to slide one panel upwards in its frame.

A sharp click reverberated around the room and seconds later a section of panelling pivoted from just below the ornate ceiling cornice, so that the bottom section snapped loose.

It immediately became clear that a complete section of panelling approximately twelve inches wide and from floor to ceiling served as a concealed entrance and exit to a hidden world.

Seconds later, Lyn squeezed through the narrow

opening and stood, covered in brick dust and cobwebs next to Anthony.

"I'm sorry it took so long, there are quite a few tunnels around this place."

Anthony pointed to a woman in the middle of the room. "But it's no surprise to you, is it, Prudence?"

By now the assembly was tiring of their relative's apparent theatrics and offered little reaction to the revelation.

"Please, there is no need for you to stand. It looks like the bang on the head you got when you slipped in the cottage is still troubling you, despite your brief visit to the cottage hospital early this morning."

The woman gave no reaction to his accusations.

"Everyone, may I introduce Dr Prudence Mayflower, visiting professor of history at Cambridge University and erstwhile collaborator with my uncle."

This time the room's attention concentrated on the stranger.

"Prudence, we know that Percy made a second call last night after I overheard him arguing with someone, which we now know to be May.

"While we cannot know what was said, we can postulate a theory which goes something like this. He told you of his discovery, expecting you to be happy for him. I suggest you played the part well, which gained an invitation for him to show you what he'd found.

"Since you brought no transport of your own, I conjecture you got a taxi. It would be an easy enough matter for the police to check the relevant records. When you arrived, Percy took you to the pigsty and entered the tunnel exactly the same way Lyn did."

Prudence Mayflower protested. "I'm too ill to deal with this nonsense and wish to leave immediately."

Anthony smiled. "I'm sure you do. However, please indulge me for a few minutes. Eventually, you arrived at his discovery. Percy was happy enough that he'd found evidence that Nicholas Owen had constructed several priest holes around the Hall in about fifteen seventy when Elizabeth the First's persecution of Catholics intensified.

"What you didn't expect to find was the body of a woman—a woman dressed from head to foot in purple, who warns the family of impending tragedy.

"But that wasn't all. That poor woman held a further secret, and I mean that literally because Percy discovered a bejewelled gold communion cup in the bones of her clasped hands.

"I'm no academic, unlike your good self. However, even I know the dangers for the family who owned the Hall at the time if Elizabeth's spies found evidence the family was still celebrating Mass."

The woman touched the wound on her forehead and momentarily closed her eyes. "You have no evidence that any of this is true. Oh, I don't mean historical fact; I refer to my part in this devious plot you imagine took place down there, wherever down there is."

Lyn took over the interrogation. "I have just come from witnessing the two saddest sights I have ever seen in my life. Percy Stanton—"

Mention of his name sent the room into an uproar. Voices shouted from all corners of the room, making deciphering any of them impossible. Eventually, Cedric's voice won the battle. "Is he..."

"Alive?" responded Lyn. "Yes... Just."

Mayflower stood rigid as the room erupted into joyous rapture.

"But that was no thanks to this lady." It took several seconds for the room to quieten as Lyn continued her explanation. "Prudence didn't care about Nicholas Owen's magnificent achievement. Once she saw the communion cup, avarice raised its ugly head.

"Percy wasn't making much sense when I found him, but I deciphered your name and the fact you hit him with the precious object, not caring whether he lived or died. The fact you were in a network of long-forgotten secret tunnels played to your advantage. Percy showed you the way in, then was rendered unconscious. It was easy enough for you to cover your escape.

"What was callous of you was to close the entrance, locking him away in a place no one even knew existed, and you almost got away with it."

The woman looked ahead again. "I did no such thing."

"If you mean not getting away with it, you're quite right. You made two gigantic mistakes. I assume greed got the better of the academic side of your brain. First, in your hurry to escape the tunnel, you bumped the communion cup on the wall and knocked one of its precious stones from its setting. I found both the damaged wall and the gem.

"Then, after slipping in the living room of the cottage and cutting your head open, you stole Percy's car and made for the cottage hospital. It was a creative touch by covering your blood up with the mat. Unfortunately for you, Detective Inspector Riley slipped on that mat early today, and I'm sure the DNA analysis will match your own.

"What you couldn't have foreseen is that even after treatment at the hospital, and despite being told not to drive, your injury overcame you. Your selfishness almost caused a second tragedy, and Dr Thorndike, on his way to the Hall to give necessary treatment to the earl, crashed into you.

How unlucky for you that the doctor recommended I brought you here to rest until the weather improved. When you woke up, the sight horrified you, no doubt thinking you were in some nightmare. Prudence, you are; but it's one of your own making."

"And then another bit of bad luck. Anthony inadvertently pressed his palm into something sharp on the cottage. floor What do you know, it was a second gem from the communion cup."

Mayflower shook her head, almost losing her balance in the process. "This has nothing to do with me, you have no evidence."

Detective Inspector Riley took up the interrogation. "Enough of this nonsense. I assume it's the bang on your head that is causing you to act so stupidly. It was a simple enough job to check who the car you drove belonged to. It's standard practice after an accident. And then there's this."

Riley moved a few paces to the cardboard box, then carefully retrieved its contents still cradled in his woollen scarf, being careful not to contaminate the evidence.

The room suddenly looked brighter as Riley held up the incredible sight of the gold communion cup, its band of diamonds sending rays of light in all directions.

"Perhaps you notice, Miss Mayflower, that there are two diamonds that had become dislodged. It will take a second to check the ones in our possession for a match. Your fingerprints will, I know, be all over this beautiful object.

Prudence erupted into a tower of rage as all pretence of innocence disappeared. "He was a selfish man, and I wish I had killed him. He agreed to show me what he'd found, but he didn't tell me about the communion cup. He kept that for himself.

"I've had a hard life, and I'll have little money to get by on when I retire. The people in this room don't understand how ordinary people live, so yes, I took the communion cup, and I almost got away with it. If it hadn't been for that stupid car accident, I'd had have been miles away.

"It would've been an easy enough job to sell the diamond separately and have the cup melted down. But guess what, these people win again."

EPILOGUE

A s the gathering in the morning room began to leave, and Riley took control of getting Prudence Mayflower back to the police station, Anthony caught sight of Dr Philpott.

"Doctor, I wonder if I might have a word?"

Philpott smiled. "I think I know what's coming."

"And so you should," said Lyn as she joined the two men.

Anthony held Lyn's hand as they neared the gentleman. "I wanted to say how indebted Lyn and I are for the superb acting job you did tonight. I thought for a moment we had pushed it too far."

The doctor's smile broadened. "What, you mean the tears? I belong to my local amateur dramatics society and tears on demand are my speciality."

Lyn pressed her free hand against his arm. "Dr Philpott, without you making the connection between the man who constructed the priest holes, Nicholas Owen, and the detailed plans Percy was looking at, we'd never have put two and two together. To say nothing of where to look. You saved

Percy's life while we were chasing our tails, it's as simple as that."

Dr Philpott's eyes lit up. "Thank you for your kind words. My only objective now is to visit my dear friend in hospital as soon as possible. We have a great deal to talk about, and an academic paper to write. Also, I have no doubt Cedric will wish to research the skull that fell from the chimney when you were playing with the children.

"You know, one of Nicholas Owen's tricks when building priest holes was to construct and paint the bricks in a dummy fireplace black to simulate burning, when the chimney was, in fact, false. That way it provided an ideal hiding place if the house was raided by Queen Elizabeth or James the First's men looking for priests.

"My bet is that the opening was later converted to a working fireplace, and for some reason we may never know, one of your ancestors got trapped in the long-forgotten priest hole."

————

As the lights dimmed in the great hall, the sound of a solo choirboy's voice echoed serenely around the hammer-beamed mediaeval roof of the spacious room.

While shepherds watched
Their flocks by night
All seated on the ground
The angel of the Lord came down
And glory shone around
And glory shone around

THE BOY'S ANGELIC VOICE LED A PROCESSION OF CHOIRBOYS and choirgirls enrobed in crisp white surplices, each holding a lit candle. As they made their way to the stage, the packed room parted down the middle to allow unencumbered progress.

Minutes later a whole assembly was happily singing carols together, as had happened every year at Stanton Hall for the previous century and a half.

"It's hot in here, Lyn. Should we get some fresh air?"

"It's freezing out there."

"Don't be nesh." Anthony gently tugged on his companion's arm as he led her through the joyous crowd and out through the French window onto an expansive snow-covered balcony.

"What an excellent end to a strange day. The villagers all together, enjoying the festivities, a white Christmas hidden from the little ones until they wake up in a few hours' time to open their presents."

They snuggled into one another and looked out over the wintry scene. Something caught Lyn's eye. "Am I imagining it or are there a couple looking at us from the treeline over there?"

Anthony looked over to where Lyn was pointing. At first, he couldn't make anything out. Then he understood. "Do you know, I think they're at peace now, don't you?"

Lyn sighed. "I think all she wanted was for someone to find her."

"And him?" said Anthony.

"He's a special man who has come home too."

"What do you mean?"

"We swapped a silver crucifix and chain for a row of wooden prayer beads. Do you know, I think he was the priest being hunted down all those years ago; somehow those two are connected. Isn't it beautiful."

"Not as beautiful as the woman I'm standing next to."

Lyn frowned. "What are you up to, Anthony Stanton?"

He smiled and reached into his pocket. Dropping to one knee, he opened a small black jewellery box and held it for Lyn to see.

"I want to spend the rest of my life with you, Lyn Blackthorn. Will you do me the honour of marrying me?"

Lyn took the ring from its box and gave Ant the broadest of smiles.

"What took you so long? Yes, of course I will."

The two lovers hugged and kissed as snow gently fell all around them, and church bells rang out to welcome Christmas day.

END

ENGLISH (UK) TO US ENGLISH GLOSSARY

- **Bit on the side:** Slang term for a mistress
- **Bobby:** A slang term for a member of police derived from the name of Sir Robert Peel, who established the force in 1829. Police officers were also known as "peelers" for the same reason
- **Buttercross:** A type of structure associated with English market towns and dating from mediaeval times.
- **Chuck:** To throw an object
- **Chuffed:** To be pleased with something
- **Chunter:** To grumble
- **Crack the flags:** Slang for a very hot day. "The sun was cracking the sidewalk."
- **Frit:** An old-fashioned and shortened way of saying "frightened"
- **Jib Door:** A door decorated/panelled to look identical to the decoration of the wall in which it is placed.

- **Jiggered:** Old English word for being tired. "After digging the garden yesterday, I'm jiggered."
- **Half cut:** Drunk
- **Lugging:** To haul an object. "I hate lugging this suitcase around"
- **Nesh:** Slang word for hating cold weather
- **Old Money:** Wealth derived from land as applied to the British aristocracy
- **Prig:** A person who is arrogant or exhibits a smug manner
- **Tanked up:** Drunk
- **Toff:** Slang word for upper class or rich person generally seen to be "looking down" on other people
- **Wherry:** A traditional sailboat used for carrying goods and passengers on the Norfolk & Suffolk Broads
- **Windscreen:** Car windshield

DID YOU ENJOY A YULETIDE MYSTERY?

Reviews are so important in helping get my books noticed. Unlike the big, established authors and publishers, I don't have the resources available for big marketing campaigns and expensive book launches (though I live in hope!).

What I *do* have, gratefully, is the following of a loyal and growing band of readers.

Genuine reviews of my writing help bring my books to the attention of new readers.

If you enjoyed this book, it would be a great help if you could spare a couple of minutes and kindly head over to my Amazon page to leave a review (as short or long as you like). All you need do is click on one of the links below.

UK
US

Thank you so much.

JOIN MY READERS' CLUB

Getting to know my readers is the thing I like most about writing. From time to time I publish a newsletter with details on my new releases, special offers, and other bits of news relating to the Norfolk Murder Mystery series. If you join my Readers' Club, I'll send you this gripping short story, plus bonus material free and ONLY available to club members:

A Record of Deceit

Grace Pinfold is terrified a stranger wants to kill her. Disturbing phone calls and mysterious letters confirm the threat is real. Then Grace disappears. Ant and Lyn fear they have less than forty-eight hours to find Grace before tragedy strikes, a situation made worse by a disinterested Detective Inspector Riley who's convinced an innocent explanation exists.

Character Backgrounds

Read fascinating interviews with the four lead characters in the Norfolk Cozy Mysteries series. Anthony Stanton, Lyn Blackthorn, Detective Inspector Riley, and Fitch explain what drives them, their backgrounds, and let slip an insight into each of their characters. We also learn how Ant, Lyn, and Fitch first met as children and grew up to be firm friends even if they do drive each other crazy most of the time!

You can get your free content by visiting my website at www.keithjfinney.com

I look forward to seeing you there.

Keith

For Joan, who is always there for me.

ACKNOWLEDGMENTS

Cover design by Books Covered

Line Editor: Paula Grundy, paulaproofreader.wixsite.-com/home

Proof Reader: Terrance Grundy, editerry.wixsite.com/proofreader

Marion

A special thank you to my wonderful advance readers group, 'Team Sleuth'.

HISTORICAL NOTE

Throughout the book I refer to Nicholas Owen as the builder of Stanton Hall's priest holes. Nicholas was a real person, a devout catholic and skilled carpenter. It is estimated he constructed around two hundred such hiding places in some of the great houses of England from around the early 1580s.

Nicholas died without revealing the names of the families who hired him to construct priest holes, or their location.

It is for this reason that even centuries after his death, his hiding places continue to be discovered... just like at the fictional home of Anthony Stanton!

ALSO BY KEITH FINNEY

In the Norfolk Cozy Mystery Series:

Dead Man's Trench

Narky Collins, Stanton Parva's most hated resident, lies dead at the bottom of an excavation trench. Was it an accident, or murder?

Amateur sleuths, Ant and Lyn, team up to untangle a jumble of leads as they try to discover the truth when jealousy, greed, and blackmail combine in an explosive mix of lies and betrayal.

Will the investigative duo succeed, or fall foul of Detective Inspector Riley?

Murder by Hanging

Ethan Baldwin hangs from a tree in woods just outside the quiet Norfolk village of Stanton Parva. The police think the respected church warden committed suicide. **Ant and Lyn are certain someone murdered Ethan and set out to bring his ruthless killer to justice.**

Suspects include a greedy land developer, a vicar in turmoil, and a businessman about to lose everything.

Can our amateur sleuths solve the crime, or will the killer get away scot-free?

The Boathouse Killer

Successful businessman, Geoff Singleton, is found dead in the cabin of his cruiser on the Norfolk Broads. His wife's ex-partner suddenly appears, and a secret which someone does not want exposed merge into a countdown to catastrophe.

When the body of a respected young entrepreneur is discovered, sat bolt upright with unseeing eyes, Detective Inspector Riley concludes it's a heart attack.

Ant and Lyn are suspicious; why would a fit man suddenly die? *The deeper they dig, the more the inconsistencies mount.* Convinced the police are wrong, the pair have just days to identify the killer before DI Riley turns on them with the threat of arrest for perverting the course of justice. *Will the killer be exposed? Or will their evil scheming pay off?*

Miller's End

Forty-five minutes ago, the owner of an ancient Norfolk windmill joked happily with his visitors. *Now he's dead. An innocent accident or murder? Time is running out to uncover the truth.*

Burt Bampton lived for his work and preserving Norfolk's heritage. How could a man used to skipping up and down the mill's narrow stairs suddenly slip and fall?

Detective Inspector Riley believes it to be a tragic accident.

Ant and Lyn think different, and as disturbing coincidences begin to emerge all the evidence points to murder. **Greed, jealousy and betrayal** take our amateur sleuths on a baffling journey to uncover the appalling truth.

www.keithjfinney.com

FACEBOOK

Created with Vellum

Printed in Great Britain
by Amazon